SHADOWS AMONG THE STARS

Rivara Fall

Book one

Shadows Among the Stars
Rivara Fall

Shadows Among the Stars
Copyright © 2025 Rivara Fall

Printed in the United States of America

Paperback ISBN: 979-8-9899296-6-5
Hardcover ISBN: 979-8-9899296-7-2
Ebook ISBN: 979-8-9899296-8-9

Edited by: Katie Bucklein
Cover design and images created by: Rivara Fall
Author Website: rivarafall.com

Chapter 1

Why am I floating out of my bed? What's going on with the gravity? A pair of blue socks floated in front of my face. *Forgot to put those away. Glad I keep my room mostly clean. Tiny desk and bed are still attached to the floor, thankfully. I'd better check control, see why my socks are on the ceiling.*

"Ah!" *Ow... Nothing like a sudden gravity shift to wake you up in the morning. Probably shouldn't have tried floating over to my closet. Dear Dad, I took a bedframe to the spine, you'll never guess how.*

I stood and ran a hand over the hangers. *Let's see, navy-blue jumpsuit, navy-blue jumpsuit, or navy-blue jumpsuit? Why not blue today? Goes well with my deep brown eyes and hair. It would be easier to get dressed if gravity made up its mind.*

I dashed out my door and turned left into the control room. *Half the screens are flashing with instability warnings and we're heading right for a small planetary body.*

A pair of small black-and-white cat plushies floated in front of my face. "Damien..."

"Emma," he responded with a smile as he placed a hand on his coffee mug, failing to keep the liquid from floating out.

1

I watched his scraggly brown hair wave atop his head. "Why are we uncontrollably careening toward an anomaly?"

He turned back toward the rapidly shifting screens and mapping holograms surrounding his station. "It's messing with the ships balance systems, throwing off our C-one and C-three distance parameter readers and causing some objects to float." He tapped one of the plushies with his finger. "Hopefully we get it figured out before we crash."

"Pull the buffer switch."

"Not responding."

"Secondary gravitational cancellers?"

"Nope."

"Fuck." I clumsily ran to the main chair and stared down at the screens. *Collision statistics are going up. At least we're not shaking around like last time.*

"Dad's going to kill us," Damien said, rushing toward a side panel.

"Only if we die."

"He was very firm about that," he said, pulling out wires. "Step one, go to space. Step two, explore uncharted galaxies. Step three, don't die. We really need to work on step three. Reeling toward an anomalous mass isn't exactly ideal."

"Wait, we're slowing down. Energy is stabilizing."

"I manually restarted the shield buffer. Systems are back online."

"Let's keep a safe distance and run some scans. We'll want to make sure we're prepared if we run into anything else giving off these signatures." I grabbed the plushies and set them back on the dash. "Maybe we should Velcro these guys down. Wouldn't want to lose them."

"Too bad we can't have the real ones. I'm sure those two would love to be out here causing mischief and chasing space anomalies."

"Moo would. I don't know about Milkshake."

"Yeah, he is more skittish. I'll close this panel, then take a look at the scanners."

I got out my tablet. "Sending a message to explain our unusual turbulence."

Damien sighed and pulled at the collar of his black jumpsuit. "I'll set the analytic computers."

"No movement. No light. Weird energy signatures we've never seen before. No wonder the scanners didn't pick it up."

"It does have an eerie feeling. Looks cool. Matte black rock with shiny dark blue veins. What should we call it?"

"The last one was Cobalt D-Five-Nine."

"D-Six-Zero, then."

"You should check with Boston, make sure the engine cores are still functioning properly."

"Don't want to do it yourself?"

"I might need to pilot us out of here if we have another problem. Besides, he's better with engines than people."

He gestured toward the symbol on my chest depicting a sun with circuitry-themed wings. "You're the captain; he sometimes listens to you. If I try to tell him anything he just looks at me like a disappointed teacher."

"Fine, but you have to deal with him next time." I stepped into the hallway and pulled out my tablet. *I should make sure everyone is still okay. Owen's in his room, probably still asleep. Damien is in control. Sophie and Eliza are in lab two. London and Kenneth, kitchen. They better not be stealing my ice cream bars again. Boston, engine room, not that he ever leaves. Hyke is in the gym. Systems are good. Gravity is stable.*

I stretched my arms and looked around at the simple grey walls. *Section one, twelve room doors, all silver with blue trim, no problems. Through the security door, section two, four common doors, more silver and blue. Break room, cafeteria, kitchen, restrooms, all good. Through another security door, section three. Storage, gym, and medical, no damage. Through one final security door to the main stairs. Hopefully Boston will be too focused on his work to mind me pestering him with questions.*

The stairs opened up into a large room containing a semi-organized mess of different metals and chemical tubing.

Let's see, short, grumpy, brown-haired man in dirty brown overalls with the void engineering gear patch poorly sewn on the front. Currently balanced on the primary engine. Right where I expected. "Why did they use so many different metals to build this thing?" I asked.

Boston lifted his head from the panel. "Titanium and stainless steel for strength and immunity to rust. The copper is best for the core fluid, but the Kethon gravity plates don't work on copper so they need to be bolted down with gold-plated screws. The core engines have to be silver and lead because of the energy source we use."

"Got it. Each metal is good for something specific. Must be a bitch to maintain."

"Only if you're lazy."

"Everything okay down here?"

"A few things started floating around. Didn't bother me. Kind of handy to have the wrench float toward you right when you need it."

"No damage?"

"Engines are perfect. Gears are clean and wires are flawless."

"How is solar charge?"

"Fine. Don't know why we need the damn things. The cores keep themselves charged at all times."

"Just emergency protocol. The new..."

"Yeah, yeah, new shit and whatever. Unnecessary hobwash. No need for all these extra fidgety things...wires are all uncoordinated..." He dipped his head into the machine, continuing to mumble.

I turned back toward the stairs. *How does he not get that stupidly long beard caught in everything? Oh well.*

Everything's fine. Better get back to control. Maybe we should just move his bed down here. Can't even count how many times I've caught him sleeping against one of the engines. Doesn't seem that safe. I wonder if he'd actually use the bed or if he'd just set tools on it.

I stopped in front of Owen's door, knocking twice. "Want to see something new, old man?"

"Always!" he responded, rustling around his room.

I swear that grey moustache of his keeps getting bushier. Maybe it just looks like that because the hair on his head is thinning.

He stepped into the hall wearing his old, faded turquoise jumpsuit. "Emma, how are we doing?"

"All good. Just a little anomaly action."

"Sounds interesting. Let's take a look." He followed me back to control, took a deep breath, and smiled. "Ah, control room sweet control room, what mysteries do you have for me today?" He stepped toward his chair and danced his fingers across the dark grey control board.

Damien turned toward him and smiled. "Hey, Owen. Decided to wear the Psych one today?"

Owen gestured toward the brain logo on his chest. "It's the most comfortable."

"I am a little jealous that you get variety."

"I worked for it."

"What colors do you have?"

"Red, grey, blue, brown, pink, and I think I still have my yellow cadet one from the old days, back at the base."

"I'm guessing it's more beat-up looking than this one."

"A bit."

"Are you going for a purple one next?"

"I'm not bossy enough to be a commander."

"No, you're not."

Owen turned toward the window. "What do we have here? Round shape, dark coloration. Seems to be emitting strange energy."

Always a look of excitement in those big hazel eyes, ready to see something new. The man has a million stories already. I hope I'm just as excited to be out here when I'm that age.

"Could be a new type of depleted star," he continued. "Those things love to give off strange types of energy."

"How many more types of stars do you think we'll discover?" Damien asked.

"Who knows. The void is showing no signs of ending. We discover new elements and weird chemical varieties all the time. Have we started getting samples from this one?"

"The girls are sending out the sample bots as we speak."

"Well, things seem to be running smooth. You two don't even need me here."

I looked at Owen. "I'll always welcome your company."

"Don't want to be stuck with only your brother to talk to up here?"

"I've heard all his stories, not yours."

"True, I am full of entertainment. I'll be heading back to bed."

Damien watched him walk out, then turned toward me. "You also going back to bed?"

"No. I was going to get up soon anyways."

"Any dreams?"

"Not last night. You?"

"I dreamt of riding horses through the void."

"Doesn't sound all that efficient."

"Nope, took forever to get anywhere."

I nodded toward the odd blue ball. "Probably would have crashed them into that dark mass."

"Yeah, I don't think Asrocore would cover medical costs for crashing a horse into an anomaly."

"You never know. The legal documents are wild."

"Wilder than anomaly protocol?" Damien asked. "Maybe we should send a copy to Dad. That'll keep him busy. Let's send one with our next update video. Dear Dad, here's all the protocol we have to learn. Keeps us on track for following step three."

"He won't understand most of it."

"We can explain it later. Ready for another day of staring at different types of rocks? Glowing rocks, plain grey rocks, rocks that look back at us funny."

I chuckled. "Dear Dad, Damien lost his mind staring at rocks."

"He'd believe it," he said, turning back toward the navigation panel.

Wake up to an anomaly, fix something on the ship, listen to one old man mumble complaints and another who's excited about everything. Make sure Damien hasn't lost his mind staring at stars all day. Typical morning in the void.

Chapter 2

It's darker than usual. No bright stars, no blue glow. I got out of bed and picked up my tablet. *Owen, Damien, Sophie, Eliza, London, Kenneth, Boston, and Hyke. All good. Systems are good. Auto lights on in four...three...two... There it goes. Jeans and a long-sleeved blue shirt should be fine. Where's my hair tie? I really need to stop losing it... Right, I put it in the drawer in case we end up getting more gravity issues. Alright, ready for another day staring at stars.* I opened my door and stared across the hall.

Damien's door beeped a few times and scraped against the floor a couple inches before sliding open.

"Morning, Emma," he said, stepping out.

"Morning."

"Did you have trouble sleeping?"

"Yeah, dreams were weird."

"Glitchy, right?"

"And pink."

"Yeah..."

"You check in with Owen in control and I'll talk to the girls, see if they know what's going on. We need to make sure these dreams aren't being caused by something hazardous."

"Alright."

"If something happens, let Owen pilot."

He grinned. "I'm never going to get better if I can't practice sometime."

"You can practice back at the base, if anyone will even let you pilot their ship."

"Fine, fine. I'm going."

Same grey walls looking exactly as they did yesterday. Down the hall, down the stairs, to the left, and into lab two. Walls covered in pristinely clean machines and science pun posters. One adorable woman with long, wavy blonde hair and a mild Canadian accent, sitting at a messy desk, and our short, brown-haired, anxiety-ridden Eliza staring at rocks. Are they still in their pajamas? Dinosaur and meteor pajamas. Adorable. "They should make these our new official outfits," I said, stepping in.

Sophie smiled and set a tiny yellow pothos plant on her desk. "They are more comfortable, though I doubt they would keep us safe in the void."

"What are you working on?"

Eliza grabbed her tablet. "Identifying samples from the D-Six-Zero anomaly. I've found a couple of new minerals that I haven't seen before. One of them seems to be what causes those dark blue colorations on the surface."

"Is it safe to touch?"

"Yes. Doesn't seem to be anything toxic."

I picked up the jagged dark blue stone from her desk. "Heavy. Its surface has a faint shine to it."

"It's similar to a metal, but I can't find its melting point with our current equipment. Seems to be able to withstand extreme cold and hot temperatures. Doesn't react to water or oxygen, but I found that it glows when it comes into contact with mercury. Haven't figured out why yet."

Sophie glared at her. "How often do you pour mercury on newly discovered rock structures?"

"Occasionally..."

"Is that bad?" I asked.

"She's a little obsessed with it," Sophie responded.

Eliza smiled. "It's a cool element."

"Until you accidentally mix it with an unknown substance and end up melting half the lab table."

"I didn't mean to...and that was over a year ago!"

"As long as you don't melt any holes in the ship," I said.

"I'm being very careful," Eliza reassured.

"So, what does this tell us about the D-Six-Zero?"

"There's a chance that the anomaly used to have a mercury core. That combined with the elements I found would seem to create a fairly strong glowing blue star, though not as bright as most."

"Owen's always right."

"How much longer are we out here for?"

"Should be done mapping our zone sometime next month."

"Then we head back to the base?"

12

"Yeah, shouldn't take long to get back. Can't wait to try out our dash systems."

"How fast can this thing go?"

"Supposed to be four times faster than the old ships, plus the advanced navigation computer. We won't need to slow down around planetary structures like we used to."

"Pretty soon we'll have colonies stretching out into the void," Eliza said, sitting down. "I'm surprised we haven't run into any other intelligent life yet with how far we've gone."

Sophie stepped closer. "We will eventually. Still don't know if space ends at any point. The stars might just go on forever."

"Sounds like an endless amount of adventures."

"And we get to be a part of it."

"Still feels weird...those moments when it really hits me how far we are from home." She stared down at her tablet. The screen was lively with chemical symbols and analytics. "My dream job is a little scarier than I imagined."

"This is probably still safer than those old training facilities."

"But nowhere near Earth."

Sophie turned toward me. "Get the map problem sorted out?"

"Yeah, everything's good," I responded. "Not that we really needed to re-scan. Damien's practically got a photographic memory when it comes to the stars."

"His sketches are crazy accurate."

13

"We've passed who knows how many stars and I have no doubt he can still direct us back to the base, probably even back to Earth without looking at the computer."

"How's everything going upstairs?"

"Smooth, aside from weird, glitchy dreams," I answered. "Both me and Damien."

"Any specific topics?"

"Pink colors. Neither of us are vivid dreamers."

"I didn't have any weird dreams, though I did spend most of the night analyzing samples." Sophie looked at Eliza. "Did you have any?"

"No visual dreams, but I did feel a bit odd, like the energy in the room was off," Eliza responded, looking back at her screen. "I'm not seeing anything obvious on the anomaly scans. Nothing that would mess with brain waves, though I'm only seeing the surface levels. They aren't reaching the anomaly's core."

"Interference?" I asked.

"The scans fluctuate depth. Whatever is interfering is moving, but our tech isn't identifying it. Possibly a new element or compound."

"Is it reacting similar to anything we do know?"

"It almost looks like a machinery signature, but more fluid."

"Machinery?"

"Yeah, most machines give off all sorts of energy fluctuations, usually in specified patterns that go along with their movements. This anomaly's waves have a pattern, and multiple overlapping signatures, but the only familiar is...maybe copper? It's faint, but there might be some in there."

"Odd for something this size to be made of almost completely unknown elements."

"Odder still for those elements to mess with our minds. Can you see if everyone had those dreams, Emma? I need to determine if it effects humans in general or just a select few individuals."

"Got it." I stepped out into the hallway. *Time to interview the crew about their dreams. I should do a routine check while I'm down here. Hallway looks good. O2 room and algae room are bright and green as always. The storage rooms are fine as well. Lab one still looks untouched. Garden is colorful; freshly watered. Power storage is fine. Armory, shiny and well-kept, not like Hyke has had many other things to do. Everything looks alright. Boston should still be down in the engine room. I can already hear him rummaging through tools. Yup, there he is, leaning into engine three.* "Boston... Boston!"

He lifted his head from the machine. "What?"

"Have you left this room at all in the past twenty-four hours?"

"Why would I? I'd have to deal with you lot bustling around talking nonsense and committing foolery."

"Fine, stay where you want. Did you get any sleep?"

"A little."

"Have any weird dreams?"

"Yeah, damn flamingoes in the engines. Darn things kept pecking at the coolant pipes and pulling on my beard."

That's hilarious... "Anything else that stood out to you?"

"It was a little fuzzy. Brain felt weird."

"How so?"

"Like energy weird. Not what I'm used to."

"Can you describe it further?"

"I don't know all that psychology nonsense. It was new and weird. That's it. Plain and simple."

Grumpy as always...

"Darn people always bothering me, asking about my dreams. Why's that got to be anyone's business?"

"Okay. I'm done asking." *I wonder if he was this stubborn and unfriendly back on Earth. The void changes people sometimes, though knowing Boston, I wouldn't be surprised if he's been this way all his life.*

I walked up the stairs and paused. *Music coming from the exercise room. Must be Hyke. Yup, tall bald man with a red Void Defense ball cap.* "Hyke."

He stopped the treadmill. "Yeah?"

"Have any weird dreams last night?"

"Yeah, actually. I was running around on a meteor, shooting flaming flamingos but the whole thing was all staticky."

Flamingoes again... "Seems a number of us had weird dreams. Eliza's having me ask around about it."

"I can head down and talk with the girls if they need."

"You just want to spend time with Sophie."

"So?"

"She isn't interested, Hyke. Give it up."

"She's warming up to me."

"Hard not to with how hotheaded you are."

"I'm efficient."

"At your job and being a pain in my ass."

"If bothering you gets us more defensive weaponry, I'll gladly keep it up."

"It's not my call, Hyke. Just do your job and stop pestering people. You can lecture the commander about it when we get back to base."

"He doesn't care enough about our defense department. We need more cadets trained in combat."

"I'm sure you've had enough combat experience to make up for a whole platoon. You've spent most of your life in training, and I'm sure you'll spend the rest of it being a stubborn soldier."

"And I'll enjoy every second of it." He turned up his music and restarted the treadmill.

Time for the next... Let's see. Someone's in the hallway. Who do we have here? Copper jumpsuit with the electrical lightbulb logo, half zipped. White tea shirt, long dark hair, tan complexion... "Kenneth? No, London. Fuck. I still can't tell you two apart from behind."

London turned and smiled, glaring at me with light green eyes. "We both keep our hair long on purpose to mess with people."

17

"Of course. How long have you been doing that?"

"Since we were kids. Even fooled our parents a few times."

"Have any odd dreams last night?"

"Yeah, everything was pink, except for the flamingoes. They were standing on the outside, watching us from the windows. It was creepy, especially since the images my head was making kept glitching out like an old computer screen."

"Weird, Hyke and Boston also dreamed about flamingos. I wonder why. We think the glitching has something to do with the anomaly. Sophie and Eliza are having me interview everyone on their dream experiences."

"Isn't that usually Owen's department? He's the one with the psych degree, and every other degree you can get out in the void."

"You can ask him what your flamingos mean later."

"I'm sure he'll have a story or two about them."

"Where's Kenneth?"

"Crawling around the outer wall maintenance shafts. He never remembers his dreams."

"Okay. I've just got to ask Owen now."

"I saw him heading toward the break room."

Alright. Down the hall, to the right, room with the TV, couch, and mini kitchen. I need to spend more time in here. The counters covered in everyone's favorite mugs, as usual. Coffee's already been started. Does anyone actually use the fancy new coffee machine in the kitchen? I only see people come in here for it.

"Emma."

And there's the old man, grey hair, mustache, sitting on the couch. Looks like he wore the pink jumpsuit today. Oddly on brand with our dream themes. His medic cross symbol looks almost like a circuitry flower. "Hey, Owen. Did you actually make that coffee or did you just steal it from someone else?"

"Not my fault they keep walking away from fresh, hot coffee."

"You're a menace."

"How is your morning going?"

"I'm doing your job today."

"How so?"

"Eliza wanted me to ask everyone about their dreams. So far, I've got a collection of weird, glitchy flamingos."

"Strange. I believe there was a flamingo in my dream as well. Just one. It was trying to fly the ship. I kept telling it to turn around, but it didn't have hands to move the controls."

"Couldn't use your own hands to help?" I asked.

"I was stuck in my chair. No idea why I couldn't get up. Just had to watch as it danced across the control panel. Did pretty well, all things considered, just couldn't turn the ship."

"That joystick is tricky."

"Yes, but far better at preventing accidents."

19

"Unless you're a bird. Have any idea why we've got recurring flamingos?"

"I don't know. No one was talking about them or watching any flamingo-based movies yesterday. The brain does weird things when exposed to new stimuli. Perhaps the energy from our anomaly causes the brain to see specific shapes or colors and our imaginations just filled in the gaps."

"No one dreamed of shrimp or pigs or any other pink birds. You'd think we might have more variety."

"We're still studying brain wave coding. Fascinating stuff. Each thing you think about causes your brain to emit a slightly different signal. They've been trying to apply it to machines and computing translations, but human brains are so finicky."

"I'll let you worry about brain waves and machine learning. My job right now is to interview people. I'll make sure to stay out of their emotions."

"Don't want a turquoise jumpsuit?" he asked.

"I've heard all your stories about how you got your psych degree, and I think I'll stick with piloting."

"You just like your jumpsuit symbol better."

I tapped a finger over the pilot symbol on my chest. "I do."

"You'll get bored of navy blue eventually."

"I'm going to report back my findings."

"Try not to trip over any flamingoes on your way down."

I'm more likely to trip over one of Sophie's plant experiments. Hope she got the two out of the breakroom stairwell. It'll be quicker if I take that one down. Straight into the lab. There they are, still staring at rocks and plants with more analytic brain cells than me and Damien combined.

"Find anything interesting?" Eliza asked, turning toward me.

"Flamingoes."

"Flamingoes?"

"Several people had dreams involving flamingoes. Boston, Hyke, London, and Owen. Kenneth doesn't remember his dreams, and mine and Damien's were less specific, mostly static."

"Interesting. Did Owen give any plausible explanations?"

"Yeah, he said they might have been a response to new stimuli. Something about different energy waves having specific effects on the brain. Our minds try to translate new input in ways we can understand. Shapes, colors. He then trailed off into research about brain wave translation and machine implications."

"Makes sense. I don't know as much about neurology, but energy is universal. How much longer are we staying near the anomaly?"

"How much longer do you need?"

"A couple more hours would be nice. I'd like to run some brain wave analytics and Kenneth was going to stop

21

by soon to talk about adapting the buffers to the D-Six-Zero."

"Okay. Send me a message when you're done. I'll be in control."

Chapter 3

Owen, Damien, Sophie, Eliza, London, Kenneth, Boston, and Hyke. All good. Systems are good. No weird anomalies at the moment. No more weird dreams. We haven't been invaded by flamingoes yet, as far as I know.

"Morning," London said, watching me step into the break room.

"How's everything holding up?"

"Good, aside from the kitchen light."

"Dislodged again?"

"Yeah, apparently it was an accident."

"A mop handle being used incorrectly again?"

"Yup."

"You'd think he'd have learned from last time. Has he fixed it yet?" I asked, pouring my coffee.

"Maybe. He keeps getting stuck in his room. I left him there earlier so he wouldn't break anything else."

I closed my eyes and set down my mug. "Alright, let's go save him."

"Do we have to?"

"We need him to stare at the stars in case the mapping system has issues."

"Fine." She turned toward a supply closet and pulled out a crowbar. "Lead the way."

If we can't fix the door, he can just sleep in Boston's room. Not like that old crotchety grump ever steps foot in it. Maybe I should toss a blanket down there for him. It's a wonder his neck still works with how many times I've gone down there and seen him hunched over, asleep on the engine. Metal can't be comfortable. Then again, he does have that long beard. That might help cushion his head a little.

London snickered as we approached the door.

"Damien..."

"Emma."

"Why is there a plastic alligator wedged in the frame?"

"London wouldn't get me a crowbar."

I reached for the door. "Alright, it should release if we pull together."

London wedged the crowbar into the frame. "Must be the emergency system malfunctioning. The bedroom doors are supposed to seal shut if we ever need to use them as life pods."

Damien laughed. "This one is just itching to keep me safe."

"Just wait until the emergency protocols fail and you get shot out into the void."

"You'd miss me."

"I don't know, I could just fool around with your sister instead."

"She's already got her eye on someone."

"Wait," I said, grabbing London's arm. "Why are the lights fading?"

The hallway went eerily quiet. No hum of electricity, not a single peep from the engines. Damien's door clicked, then slid open. A faint blue glow filled the air.

"Looks like we lost power," London said, looking up at the glass tubes that ran along the corners between the walls and ceiling. Various shades of aqua and blue swirled through them, providing soft shifting light. "At least the emergency bio panels are still glowing."

"Maybe there's a problem in the control room," Damien suggested.

London grabbed her flashlight. "We have three engines on their own circuits. Engines one and three are programmed to stay active if there's a computing malfunction. They couldn't all have gone off at once."

"Something has to be wrong somewhere," I said. "Let's head to control."

Damien followed us through the door, stopping at his station. "Solar isn't working either. Not sure if it's the panels or something else."

"When did we last test them?" I asked, standing in front of my chair.

"Just under a week ago. They were fine. We haven't hit anything and we're too far from a sun to get a solar burst."

"I'm surprised it's not obvious. A problem this severe, you'd think something would have happened. The sensors were all fine. We're far enough from that last anomaly."

"Are the buffers still on?"

"No, we're completely dark. Luckily, we're not floating toward anything."

"Maybe we hit another anomaly. These are uncharted areas. Anything could be out here. Are personal electronics off as well?"

I pulled out my tablet. "Mine is still working. Full charge."

"So, whatever is going on has to do with the ship itself," London noted. "We can't stay dark for long. Can we send out our emergency beacon?"

"No," I responded. "It's on the outside of the ship. Can't activate it manually."

"That's an incredibly dangerous design choice."

"I don't think we've ever had a ship lose power like this before. We've always been able to rely on solar or emergency reserves. Even in exigency situations, we're still supposed to have power in the control room. Communications, at least."

"Exigency?"

"Another word for emergency."

"Oh. Well, it is a new ship, new systems, new malfunctions."

"Morning, evening, or afternoon, I'm not sure," Owen said, walking in. "Boston has no idea why we're dark, said everything was running perfectly before it happened. He's a regular old engine room gremlin. He would know if anything was wrong. How are the oxygen reserves?"

"Still full," I responded, checking my tablet. "I'll give everyone a notice to get into their jumpsuits just in case and start doing a large scale eval."

"Is anyone unaccounted for?"

"All vitals are normal. The girls are in the lab. Eliza just reported that they have no power down there, either. Kenneth is crawling around the maintenance tunnels. Hyke is still in his room. We're all good."

"No point in panicking. I'll start checking the wiring at the back of this room. Stay at your station, Emma. Let me know if anything turns on. Hopefully this is a temporary issue."

"Alright."

London grabbed her tablet and sat in Owen's chair. "I'm not getting any readings from the ship. We haven't been in contact with anyone else and the programming was running smooth. No code malfunctions."

"Can you still see the codes from your tablet?" I asked.

"Yes. I always have a copy in case something on the ship needs reprogrammed. I'll take a closer look, but a total failure like this when we're completely alone out here is strange. I don't think it's a coding problem. Especially since the different main departments are running on separate systems. The labs, the engines, the control room, and oxygen room are all separate in case of emergencies."

Damien stared out the window. "No one saw anything, we're all accounted for, all systems were fine, and there's no other ships around to sabotage. What the hell happened?"

"A mystery," Owen said, opening one of the maintenance panels. "I'm sure we'll be alright. One of my first ships, the *Star Shark*, lost power. Not to this extent. It was a prototype. First in the line of new velocity ships capable of traveling far faster than the old frontier ships. I was taking a shower, then everything went dark. The red emergency lights turned on. Glad I had already rinsed the soap out of my hair. Took them six days to make and ship us a new part for the core engine. Wasn't the worst situation. We still had limited power from the solar panels. Came up with all sorts of games with whatever we could find, though it was a little tricky in zero gravity."

"The gravity failed?"

"This was a few years before we discovered Kethon. I remember seeing it in the news. Reginald Kethon discovers a new element bringing advancements to space travel. Everyone was excited to be done with the old gravity simulating systems. It did take them a while to figure out how to fit it to ships for use in space travel. You have to have just the right amount of Kethon to replicate Earth's gravity."

"Glad it doesn't need power to work."

"I had a guy get stuck outside the ship once before they invented buffer shielding. Roger Laroy, great engineer. He was out trying to fix one of our external lights. Me and Ron accidentally hit the airlock door with a recliner, bent the hinge. He could come in, but the emergency protocol wouldn't let the room fill with oxygen because the door was broken."

"Why were you moving a recliner?"

"Barbara broke the ice cream machine in one of the break rooms, soaked the floor, so we moved a few things to one of the other break rooms. We spent the next three hours trying to fix the door and the ice cream machine. Vessels weren't as sturdy when I was young."

"Have you ever been on one of the space cruise ships, Owen?" London asked.

"No, actually. One of the few lines of ships I haven't worked with. Not all that exciting really, especially when you've been out to space as many times as I have. A fancy resort circling Earth. Not much adventure."

"They're good intro ships, especially for kids. My grandparents took me and Kenneth on one when we were younger. First time in space. Had a blast, especially when we discovered they have pools and hot tubs. You can swim among the stars."

I smiled. "Bet that would have been fun on an older ship, one with gravity simulation instead of Kethon. The gravity fails, water starts floating everywhere. All the damage it would cause. Guess that's why ships aren't allowed to have bathtubs."

"We have Kethon," London said. "Maybe we should request a bathtub. It would help with relaxation."

"We deal with anomalies. Just had an incident with gravity failure two days ago."

"Right... See anything, Owen?"

He closed the panel. "Nothing. My guess is that our evaluation software is faulty. We might have had a serious issue that it didn't pick up."

I stood and tucked my tablet into my belt. "Alright, everyone head to your emergency section. Look over every inch of the ship. Try to use the tablets only when necessary. We need to conserve power in case this lasts a while."

"Got it," London said, stepping out.

Damien sat on the floor and opened the central panel. "Watch it be something diminutive."

"Or minuscule," I added, glaring at him.

"Microscopic."

"Nanoscopic."

"Titchy."

"Bitty."

"Measly."

"Runtish."

Owen shook his head and took a sip of coffee. "You going to do that until you run out of words again?"

"Maybe," Damien answered. "Hold on...that's my coffee."

Owen grinned. "Not anymore."

"Both of you get back to evaluating," I said, getting out a small tool kit. "Less lollygagging. We need efficiency, not foolery."

Owen shined a flashlight toward the poster on the wall depicting two black-and-white cats sitting on a windowsill showing a colorful galaxy behind them and the words *Felis Regere Universum* above. "Do you really think I'd do anything to disgrace those two?"

"No one would dare disgrace them."

He saluted the poster before walking out.

Damien stood. "I'm sure the ship wouldn't dare lose power if the cats were on board."

"Because the universe obeys cats?"

"Everything else does, why not the void?" He grabbed a small tool. "Hope the issue isn't in one of the core wires. Those things aren't easy to get to."

"Kenneth can handle that."

"He's pretty catlike. Always crawling around the maintenance vents, gets excited by flashing lights, knocks things off counters, likes rats. London told me they had a pair of pet rats when they were in training. Waffle and Pancake."

"Why are so many animal pairs named after foods?"

"I don't know. We've been naming a lot of constellations after them lately."

"Because you're always hungry."

"It's going to be a long day, isn't it?"

"Very."

Chapter 4

"Glad Owen always keeps his old-fashioned manual coffeemaker on hand," Damien said, reaching for his mug.

I leaned against the counter. "I'm surprised Boston hasn't drank it all by now."

"I don't think I've seen him today."

"Probably fell asleep in the engine room again."

"He still doesn't like me."

"Maybe you and Kenneth should stop sword fighting with mop handles."

"We didn't mean to break anything..."

"Like the kitchen light?"

A look of guilt came over his face as he grabbed the sugar.

"We're going to run out of lightbulbs if you keep it up."

"We were bored. Besides, it's good to keep up with combat training."

"Sure."

"You never know, we could run into sword-wielding aliens."

"Sword-wielding aliens?"

"Would make a pretty badass story."

"True."

Kenneth burst through the door. "We're sealing off the lower-level doors, keeping access to the labs only."

"What? Why?" I asked.

"Boston's dead. Eliza found him by the second engine."

"How'd he die?"

"He has a large wound across his chest. She couldn't find any obvious cause. Said it looked recent. They're going to stay in the lab until they can make sure there isn't any contagious illness or biological anomaly on board."

"Is anyone else down there?"

"No."

"Damien...shit we don't have power. Let's head to control, let Owen know. Kenneth, continue with the doors." I stepped into the hallway, glaring down at my tablet. *Owen's in control. Damien's with me. Sophie and Eliza, lab two. London, kitchen. Kenneth, hallway. Hyke, upstairs storage. Boston... Boston's tablet is down. Why the hell didn't I get a notification? No alerts, nothing. Settings are fine. What the hell?*

"What's wrong?" Owen asked, watching us rush through the door.

"Boston was killed," I responded. "Kenneth is sealing the lower access doors aside from the labs. The girls are running manual eval scans and we're still powerless."

"What happened to him?"

"Large cut across his chest."

"I'll take a look after the girls are done evaluating."

"Everyone else is fine, as far as I know. My tablet didn't alert me to any issue with Boston. No alert, no emergency call, nothing."

"Is it still on?"

"No, his is dark."

"The tablets don't always alert low power. It could have died because he forgot to charge it. He's done it before."

"I didn't check power levels on everyone's tablets. Shit."

"Calm down, Emma. We need to rationalize this. He could have fallen off an engine and cut himself open. We don't exactly have lights on at the moment."

"Eliza would have been able to tell if that were the case. She would have looked for blood on the machines."

"It was a large wound?"

"Yes."

"Then perhaps you're right. There would have been a lot of blood on whatever got him. Do we know how long he was dead for?"

"Eliza said the wound looked fairly recent."

Damien looked concerned. "Should we worry about sabotage?"

"I don't think anyone on board would try to kill us," I responded.

"Maybe we have a secret invisible assassin. We have the technology."

"We're not in a movie. Besides, who would want to take out an exploration crew?"

"Those weirdos who think we need to stay on our original planet. Or maybe an intelligent alien race that doesn't want us wandering into their business."

"Problem with the void, anything could have happened. Science, physics, gravity, can all fly out the window in a heartbeat out here."

"Exactly, space assassins could be a thing. Maybe we disturbed something or look delicious."

I turned toward him. "Eaten by invisible space aliens would be a hell of a story."

"A great opening for our next message home. Dear Dad, we got eaten."

"I can practically hear him yelling, 'What happened to step three?'"

"Well, step three to us is not dying. Maybe step three to an alien is cook the human thoroughly or cover with space garlic. Would they cook us with fire or some alien tech?"

"We'll have to ask when we get captured." I looked down at my tablet as it beeped. "Eliza's done with evaluations. I'll meet them in the break room. Damien, stay here in case something changes with the power."

"Okay. Yell if something happens."

Owen followed me out.

I ran to the break room. *It'll be safer for them to use the secondary stairs. Hope they're okay. I imagine Eliza's having a hard time with it. It's never easy finding a body, especially someone you know... The door is opening. They both look pretty shaken.* "You okay?"

"Yeah," Eliza responded, nervously sitting on the couch. "I didn't find any traces of illness. We should be good. We're lucky the portable analyzers still had power."

"What happened?"

"Not sure. I went to look for Boston. He wasn't responding. Saw blood on the floor. Followed it to him. Saw a big slice on his chest. Looked around, couldn't find a cause, checked for a pulse, then ran back to warn everyone."

"Did he get cut on the machinery?"

"I don't think so. There wasn't anything on the engine. He was just lying there in a pool of blood. The cuts weren't sharp enough for a knife, looked more like he was torn open with something more jagged. We should have Owen take a look."

"We don't know enough about what happened. I don't want us losing our only medic." I turned toward the hallway door. "Hyke?"

"Yes?" He walked in with large rifle in his hand. His dark red defense jumpsuit was covered in equipment: gun holsters, ammo belts, and a thicker bulletproof material covering his chest.

"Escort Owen down to evaluate Boston's body."

Hyke loaded his rifle and slowly entered the stairwell. Owen followed close behind.

My eyes affixed to the door. *No power, no sound... I hadn't noticed how silent the ship is. The typical electrical hum, the sound of Hyke's music blasting out of the gym,*

36

people chatting in the break room, playing video games. The only sound now is the gentle tap of Sophie's fingers against the countertop.

"Look outside, watch the stars. No matter where you are, they'll stun you with their beauty. Nothing is a greater distraction than the stars."

You were right, Mom.

Sophie sat down. "They've been down there for a while. Hope it's going well."

I leaned on the couch next to her. "They have to analyze, move him to the morgue, and check the lower floor, slow and careful."

"Hyke, being careful?" She smiled.

"Well, sometimes."

Footsteps rushed up the stairs. Hyke ran to the sink, running water over his face.

"What happened?" I asked.

Owen dashed in and shut the door. "We were able to get his body to the morgue. Looked like something large slashed into him, possibly bled to death. We saw something moving down there, just for a moment, then one of the engine coolant pipes burst open, got Hyke in the face."

"Those pipes wouldn't just burst with no power..."

"No, they wouldn't."

"You and Kenneth check the other two lower access doors. We need to find out where these things are. Hopefully they got sealed in the engine room."

London looked nervous. "Something's on the ship? How? We don't have void access. The only door on and off is programmed to seal shut while we're out here."

"I'm not sure," I responded. "We don't know anything about it, what it's made of, how long it's been here."

"It couldn't have just materialized out of nowhere. We haven't landed anywhere, and we haven't been in contact with anything since..."

"The supply ship. Boston said it didn't look like it was running properly. Their power was faulty."

"They stop all over the place, meet up with other exploration vessels, and they have less strict boarding procedures than us. Anything could have snuck onboard."

"Could whatever is on our ship be messing with the power?"

"If it is, I'm not sure how it's doing it."

Hyke looked uncertain. "Do we really think these things could be causing the outage?"

"Could be," London responded. "We don't have any other idea why our power drained completely."

"We saw something move below and you're immediately assuming it's some kind of power-absorbing alien?"

"There's nothing wrong with our power. No damage or flukes in the programming. The ship is fine aside from the known comm and camera issues, but those wouldn't kill our power. It should be running properly."

"Just seems like we're jumping to conclusions."

"We're hypothesizing causes for our problems," Sophie said. "I wonder where it's originally from, and how it got onto the supply ship. Hope that crew is doing alright. Won't know until we get power back on and get out of here. I hope these things aren't spreading between ships. This could be a bigger problem than we realize."

"The supply ships only go to specified locations. Shouldn't be too hard to find, even if they go dark."

"What's the usual protocol for when things get on board?" Eliza asked.

I sat down. "First is to try and contain the life form in one space. Second is evaluating for contaminants and securing the safety of the crew. Third is to try forming communications. If they are friendly and won't end up accidentally killing us, we can open access and establish friendship. If they aren't friendly, cannot be communicated with, or can cause potential disease, we have to get them off the ship."

Eliza stepped closer. "They didn't finish my group's training. We were supposed to train for two more weeks before being deployed. Asrocore was being pressed to send more ships out, so they assigned us early. I don't know all of the emergency protocols..."

"Not the best choice Asrocore ever made."

"Our visitor or visitors are clearly hazardous. We don't have functioning comms on board. I don't know how we're going to get them off. We don't have an airlock room."

"Our only choice is to contain them, figure out what they are, and how to isolate them to a room. Then we can see if we can communicate."

Damien stepped in. "Ask them if they like popcorn."

"We're out of popcorn," I said.

"Oh."

"We should start thinking of containment ideas, how we are going to adapt our safety protocols and figure out a resource rationing system in case we end up still for too long. We should have an extra month's worth of food. It needs to work."

"Unless our new friends are tasty. Dear Dad, we cooked an alien today. Really good when fried in olive oil."

Eliza giggled. "I don't know if we should try eating strange things just yet."

"Yeah," Sophie agreed, "You wouldn't want to catch an alien disease that keeps you from making jokes all the time."

"Anything for science."

I nudged his shoulder. "Back on topic. You should plan a manual map in case we have to pilot without assistance. Hyke, get some rest. Sophie and Eliza can start on the ration plan. London, wait for Owen and Kenneth to return. I'll head to control."

Chapter 5

Break room is empty. Good time to get coffee. Looks like someone already started it. Let's see, cat mug, cat mug, or cat mug? Let's go with the one with Milkshake on it today. They never seem to get the eyes wide enough on his merch. He looks too normal.

I reached for my mug, taking a sip. *Better keep this close. Don't want Owen stealing it. Speaking of...*

"Finished my report for Asrocore," he said, walking up to me.

"What's your analysis on Boston?"

"Something unknown tore into him. Etched into his ribs. One quick, efficient blow. Died quickly. Haven't been able to find any sort of weapon that matches his wound, though I doubt anyone on our crew would attack someone."

"I don't believe anyone did it."

"Neither do I, but protocol is protocol, and every option must be explored."

"Did you put together a statistics list, then?"

"Yes, and statistically, even with the grumpy, hotheaded, and goof-off crew we have, we don't have any potential suspects."

"Expected."

"Perhaps we'll get more answers from our biological findings. Is Sophie still analyzing Boston's blood samples?"

"Not sure. Let's check." I turned and headed down the stairs. *Looks like they got one of the emergency lanterns set up. Not as bright as the main lights, but much better than the rest of the ship.*

Sophie sat at her desk, holding a flashlight. Her dark green eyes were focused on a small vial of blood.

"Get anything on Boston's scans?" Owen asked.

She handed him her tablet. "His cells are degraded more than I expected for how long he's been dead. The mitochondria are heavily damaged. Other than that, his blood was normal. No infections, unusual substances, or toxins."

"Strange, he didn't have any diseases or conditions that would have caused this. He was sliced open, and something caused cell failure, almost like his body was drained of energy."

I looked at the screen. "So whatever is down there not only drained our power but Boston as well?"

"It would seem so," Owen answered. "If it is a creature, I wonder if it drained him first so he would be easier to take down. Or it could have been the opposite. If they attacked and killed him so they could drain his cells." He turned toward Sophie. "Did you find any sign of a living organism in the engine room?"

"No, though we weren't looking for one before Boston was killed."

"I don't feel like we have enough information to go into that area safely. We should just observe what we can from here."

"Hard to be excited about finding potential alien life when you have a fatality. I honestly thought we'd find more life on planets, not out in the void."

I shrugged. "Space is strange."

She smiled. "Put that on a poster."

Owen looked down at his tablet. "London is requesting assistance. I'll leave you two to explore theories. Try not to get drained or eaten."

I placed a hand on his shoulder. "I'll just start rambling about space travel facts like you do in hopes that it bores them to death."

"Anything to follow step three." He turned and left.

Sophie grinned. "Maybe those flamingoes we were dreaming about manifested on the ship."

"Deadly energy-absorbing flamingoes? You're just as creative as Damien. He suggested invisible alien assassins."

"Maybe we should start betting on our ideas."

"Are you sure your funny little void plant hasn't grown legs and is plotting to overthrow us?"

She grabbed the larger pot on her desk. "Still here, just as I left it."

Its leaves were a dark greyish blue with bright, glowing aqua veins lined with speckles. The leaves at the top were triangular with rounded edges. One point longer than the rest. The ones below were small and circular with a dark green surface.

"Kenneth suggested I name it Clarence," she said.

I raised an eyebrow. "Clarence?"

"After the botanist who worked on the first void exploration ship."

"How's it doing?"

"It seems to like the new soil we made. Eliza added a few extra minerals."

"Remember when you found that thing? You were so excited."

"It's rare to find living specimens on meteors, aside from simple cell organisms."

"That was an eventful day. Dodging meteors, discovering plant life."

"It's grown pretty fast. It was less than an inch tall when we found it."

I looked closer. "Still looks fairly harmless compared to some of the stories Owen told me."

"It doesn't have any mutation phase genes as far as I could tell. Should just stay an ordinary...well, a simple bioluminescent space plant."

"Glad to know it's not going to start leaking toxic chemicals. Owen still gets a wild look in his eyes every time he tells the story about his void plant findings."

"If it does, we can throw it into the unknown substances isolation room." She set the pot in her lap and looked out the window.

A faint glow of light shined in from the stars outside.

"Are we moving?" she asked.

"Slowly."

"What time is it?"

"Nine fourteen back where I'm from."

"Wonder what's going on back home."

"Most people are probably in bed. A few night owls waking up."

"It felt weird waking up this morning, not having the automatic day-night cycle lights. Hope we can fix the power before anything comes our way."

"Three anomalies back-to-back would be a bit much."

"Have you named all these constellations yet?"

"Just one." I pointed straight ahead. "Blueberry muffin."

"You seem to be naming a lot of them after foods lately."

"It's been way too long since I've had a muffin."

"Not brave enough to try baking?"

"Nope. Maybe I'll ask Kenneth to make some. It'll be a good distraction for him. I know he's been running nonstop around the ship since the lights went out."

She glanced down at the floor. "It's still hard to believe. I know it's dangerous out here, but...I guess I didn't expect someone to die, especially with how well things were going."

"The first exploration ship I was on had a brace door failure. It was small, the scans didn't pick it up. Didn't realize that oxygen was leaking until four people passed out in the loading dock. We were only able to save two of them."

"You're a little more adjusted to this than I am."

"There's less you can control in space. Each year they come up with new tech to make it safer. We're probably on one of the safest ships that exist right now."

"I'm still a little scared."

"We'll be okay. I'm sure Owen's survived worse."

"Emma..." She paused and turned toward me. "The ship has isolation commands for the power, right?"

"Yeah."

"What if we isolate power to one section at a time? Then we can see if the problem is in a specific area."

"Brilliant, Sophie. I'll try shutting off power in the main lower sections where we're having strange activity. Isolate the control room, upper floor, and this lab. Let's see if we can get some power restored."

She followed me up the stairs, through the break room, down the hall, and into control.

I ran to the small, cramped utility closet at the back of the room, analyzing the large, color-coded switches and fuses that lined the wall. *Wait, where are the gloves? Right, we're dead. No need to worry about getting electrocuted. I still need to ask Damien where he put them.* "Watch the control panel for me," I said, disconnecting the lower-level fuses.

"How long do you think it will take?" she asked, stepping toward my station.

"Could be instant if the power supply picks back up. If we have to rely on solar recharge, then it will take much longer."

"I'm not seeing anything so far."

"Damn, guess we have to wait for solar."

"We can always ask Owen to tell us about another one of his adventures to pass the time."

"I can tell you a few if you'd like. He told me one the other day about a woman who accidentally made herself glow in the dark."

"How...?"

"She was a chemist who accidentally poured nontoxic glowing paint into her bottle of soap instead of the moisturizer she made. It was the same color, and she was in a rush. Next morning, Owen heard mad giggling from her room. Her roommate woke up to a weird glow."

"Is she still glowing?" Sophie asked.

"No, it wore off, but it did give them ideas for Halloween."

"I wonder if Eliza and I could figure out how to make that stuff. Everything made by Asrocore employees is uploaded to our main filing systems."

"He has a few other stories about the same woman. Apparently she was known for working unreasonable hours, not getting enough sleep, and ending up in a variety of odd situations."

"Like?"

"Making socks that stay hot constantly, eating a three-hundred-year-old plant seed because she dropped it in her trail mix, accidentally turning her gloves into Jello, and I think she's the one who invented those edible peanut butter candles."

"I'm sure she sends the wildest update videos to her family."

"Well, our line of work gives plenty of story opportunities to people in all different fields."

"I get the plant seed and the candles, but I have no idea how her gloves turned to Jello."

"Neither did she."

Chapter 6

I laid in my bed, staring at the old analogue clock on the wall. *Glad that thing has its own power. Just past four in the morning back home. Dad's asleep. Rhonda is probably up watering her flowers. Bob won't get up until noon...Three knocks. Must be Damien.*

The door slid open, revealing his tired face and partially unzipped black jumpsuit with a compass symbol on the chest. "Can't sleep either?" he asked.

"No."

I stood and stretched my arms. "Let's go check the power, see if anything changed." *I should check vital stats... Let's see. Owen's in his room. Damien is in the hallway. Sophie and Eliza are in Sophie's room. London and Kenneth, break room. Hyke is in lab one, probably keeping an eye on the other lower access door. Boston... Boston's in the morgue. Alone. At least he liked being alone. I'd better make sure no one disturbs him. Don't want to lose anyone else.*

Damien walked to the power panel at the back of the control room. "Ten percent power," he said.

I ran to my seat. The lights slowly flickered on. "We have power to the main panel. Run a diagnostic. We have to make sure the controls are working properly."

Damien sat in his chair and flipped a switch. Several bright screens and navigation holograms booted up around him. "Solar panels are working. Diagnostics clear, not that its accurate."

"This means the power drain isn't coming from the control room."

"It's got to be in the engine room."

"Do we have enough power to test the lights?"

"We should." Damien touched a small panel. The lights flickered on. "We should call a meeting. We'll need to plan our power usage."

"London, Kenneth, and Hyke are already up, and I doubt Eliza is getting much sleep with her anxiety."

"Okay. I'll get everyone gathered."

Maybe the good news will help settle their minds. We haven't solved our issue, but we're making progress. Progress is key in the void, at least that's what Owen's old posters say. Progress and good snacks. Maybe we can get the power high enough to have Kenneth bake those muffins.

Six tired faces followed Damien back into control.

Owen's wearing the red one today, matching Hyke. Defense logo hasn't changed much over the years. Owen's shield is missing the second white border, but the sun in the middle is the same. Hyke's got his weird hybrid blaster rifle thing.

Sophie sat next to me and leaned against my shoulder. "It's getting cold."

"Good excuse to stay close," I said, putting an arm around her.

"If only we'd stopped just a little closer to a sun or packed some hand warmers."

"It should heat up soon," Damien said. "We were able to get limited power on this floor. Lights and emergency equipment are functional."

"No power below?" Hyke asked, adjusting his hat.

"Lab two has power. I'd rather not risk adding too many lower rooms just yet."

London stepped closer. "Good. We'll need a lab to help figure out what's on board, and why they coincided with our power outage."

"We should wait to use any of the major equipment until we get to at least twenty percent," Damien added. "The labs use up a lot of power."

"How fast is it charging?"

"Two percent an hour or so. It isn't very consistent. We need to watch power usage. Short showers. No video games. I'll see if I can get lights on in the green rooms. Hope the plants aren't suffering too much from their days in the dark."

"The rest of us need to be aware of lower access doors," I said. "Check on them regularly. If you see something unusual, let us know. Limit your time alone for safety."

Hyke tapped his rifle on the floor. "We should start reclaiming the lower level."

"How?" I asked. "We don't even know what we're up against."

"We shouldn't just sit around, waiting for something to happen."

"We can't arm ourselves; the armory is in the dark zone."

Damien gestured under my seat. "The emergency control weapon."

"We can save those," Hyke said. "I have two more guns in my room, all fixed with flashlights. Whatever is down there could be damaging our ship. What if something happens in the oxygen room? We need to regain access to the lower level."

"Fair point. Owen?"

He sat in his chair and rubbed his chin. "It's risky, but we might have to. Oxygen and food are potentially at risk."

"Fine. One room at a time. We'll set up a team. Owen, Hyke, and I will go down. Don't shoot anything unless you have to." *I was just getting comfortable....* I stood and handed Sophie a blanket. "Keep it warm for me?"

"Only if you promise to come back in one piece."

"I'll do my best." I turned toward Hyke. "Let's get armed."

He led us down the hall and opened his door. "Trying to get all cozy with her, Emma?"

"Comfort isn't a crime."

"It can be in the world of fashion crimes," Owen said with a smirk.

I stopped and stared at Boston's door across from Hyke's. *You might have been less grumpy if you actually slept in a bed, old man.*

Hyke stepped into his room and grabbed the two guns off his desk, nearly knocking a stack of pictures onto the floor.

Those must have been from his training days. Smiling faces holding experimental weapons in front of a void testing range. I remember using one of those. Damien got way too excited about the zero-gravity target practice.

"Here, loaded and ready," Hyke said, handing them over. "Trigger is a little sensitive on these models. Dual core energized bullets in Owen's mid-length blaster, and singular stunner bullets in your handgun, Emma."

I honestly don't even remember what dual core means... "Hope they work against our visitors. We'll go through the secondary stairwell, lab two, try to make a path toward the back of the ship, get more weaponry and recheck the engines."

"Perhaps we should check the oxygen room," Owen said, walking back down the hall. "Arming ourselves is pointless if we can't breathe."

I stepped into the break room. "Fair, but we won't be able to fix much in the O-room without power. Need the water pumps to work to get the chemical conversion, and with no light we can't help the plants, either."

"Alright." He stopped in front of the stairway door and turned toward me. "Ready when you are, Captain."

This is a weird feeling. I used to be the one taking orders from him. He's looking at me like he has all the confidence in the world I'll lead them well. Time to face our shadows.

Hyke adjusted his gun. "Ready."

"Go slow," I said, stepping forward. *Step three... Step three...*

Hyke pulled the manual lock and slid the door open.

I stared down the stairs, lit by the dim blue bio lights. *This is the first time I wish the doors were louder. Anything to stop the piercing silence that's flooding my ears. There's nothing like the endless silence of a calm void. We always had the hum of our machines, the basic sounds of life, movement. Okay, Emma. Survival training, combat regulations, anomaly adaptation techniques. Make sure I'm in the right mindset.* I began my decent.

The room filled with shifting lights giving oddly shaped shadows to lifeless machines.

The lantern is still on. Doors still sealed. Nothing out of place.

"Stay close but not too clumped," Hyke said. "We don't want to risk being taken out all at once."

Owen grabbed hold of the manual door latch. Again, the quiet was disturbed by the sound of metal sliding smoothly across a track followed by the soft patter of footsteps as he stepped forward and turned to the right. "Clear."

Hyke followed, turning left. "Something moved down in the engine room. At least our height."

"Which way did it go?"

"Toward engine one. Must be moving carefully. I didn't hear anything."

I stood between them. "Follow. Owen, keep an eye on the other end of the hall. I'll close the door behind us." *You'd expect even an alien stowaway would make some kind of sound. Everything that moves does. It makes me realize how many things are still automatic for us. We expect sound because we're used to it. Another rule of human life that means nothing in the void.*

The flashlights flickered.

Hyke stopped just inside the engine room. "Hold on, these things aren't connected to anything. They shouldn't be draining."

"The bio lights are still on," I said. "We'll slow down. Communicate immediately if you feel anything strange." *Looks creepy down here in the dark. I'm sure Boston would still know his way around those engines without the light. He never came up when the power dropped, did he? Never scared, always ready to get shit done.*

"Wait," Owen said, staring to the left. "What's that on the armory door frame?"

Hyke stepped closer to him. "Owen, turn your gun back on."

"What?"

"It's powered down."

"I didn't turn it off..."

A large shadow shoved him against the wall.

"Owen!" Hyke fired his weapon, lighting the air with bright red streaks of color.

The creature darted into the power storage room.

Fuck, they are about our size. Bipedal. Still didn't hear anything, it just showed up—wait, something's moving to the left. Shit, my gun's not working, either. "Hyke, behind you!"

He turned and shot toward another shadow.

I grabbed Owen's arm. "Everyone back to the lab."

"Get the door resealed," Owen said, stumbling in.

Hyke slid it closed and secured the lock.

I kneeled next to Owen. "Were you able to get a good look at it?"

"No, it was too dark." He looked at Hyke. "Did you hit it?"

"Affirmative, but nothing dropped. They just kept moving."

I nodded toward the door. "Keep an eye on it. I'll get Owen upstairs."

Owen's legs wobbled beneath him. "Good thing I wore the red one today."

I glanced toward the growing patch of darkening fabric on his shoulder. *We're all still alive. Only one injured and we got a little more information.*

Owen's breathing shifted with each step. "At least we still have the lab. Wish we could have done more."

I reached for the latch, pushing the door open.

"What happened?" London asked, watching me set Owen on the couch.

"Something attacked him. We saw two separate shadowed figures."

"What did it look like?"

"I don't know," Owen responded. "The hallway was too dark. The lights started failing shortly after we opened the door. I just saw movement, then felt a sharp pain in my arm."

"They're upright," I added. "About our size. That's all I could get from the moments of light sparking from Hyke's gun. Mine and Owen's powered down when the lights failed."

London grabbed the weapons out of our hands. "I can take a look, see if I can get them working again. Only having one isn't ideal."

I turned toward Kenneth. "Head down and help Hyke keep an eye on that door. Hopefully whatever these things are can't open them."

"Got it."

"Alright, Owen, let's get you to medical."

"I can still walk, you know."

"I still want to make sure you don't pass out on our way there. We don't know if that thing infected you with anything. Looks like it was able to tear through the suit."

"Impressive considering what this is made of. Might need a classic suit of metal armor for this occasion. Not normally practical out here, though I might know a woman who smuggled a full suit out to a station. Wears it for Halloween and Origins Day. Heavy and uncomfortable but looks cool."

"I'm guessing you helped her smuggle it out here?"

"Maybe..."

"Here, sit down and let's stop that bleeding." *Where is that flashlight... By the door? Nope, on the counter.*

"The wound isn't too big. It feels weird, though."

"How weird?" I asked, rummaging through the drawers.

"Weak...sore...like I just used it all day and the muscles are out of energy. Hand me the portable analyzer."

"Here."

"Let's see what my cells say." He held the device over the wound. It beeped slowly for a few seconds before the screen flashed. "Help me stop the bleeding while I look at the results."

I grabbed the med kit and unzipped the top of Owen's jumpsuit exposing his old, faded blue academy shirt. "You're going to have to toss this, old man."

"I've had this thing for years! It's comfortable."

I helped him pull it off. "I can see that, but now this sleeve is covered in blood, and whatever contaminants came off that creature."

"I refuse to give up on it. I've gotten anomalous substances out of this shirt before."

"What's the scanner saying?"

58

"Nothing foreign. No odd cells, potential disease or viruses. No broken bones, though I am having trouble moving it. Seems my mitochondria are damaged, just like Boston. It's going to take a while until I can use this arm again. Might end up with permanent functional limitations. Hard to recover if my cells can't produce energy properly. We'll put it in a sling once you're done cleaning and bandaging me up."

"I'm not the best at this. Maybe we should have had one of the girls do it."

"You're just fine, Emma. It's not the first time you've had to patch me up."

"True, but I didn't need a scientific analytic eye to help you after you tripped and fell into a supply crate. The girls might see something I don't."

"Something the analyzer didn't?"

"Fair point. Here, I'll position the sling. Get comfortable."

He shifted his arm and adjusted the straps. "Alright, that should be fine. I'm good as new."

"Take a break. Get some rest."

"Alright, Captain."

I stepped out into the hallway and pulled out my tablet. *Glad the trackers are still working. Owen's in medical, Damien and London are in the break room. Kenneth and Hyke, lab two. Eliza and Sophie are back in the control room. I should check on them. Boston's still in the morgue... Still alone.*

I walked to my room and pulled off my suit, staring at the stain of fresh blood. *I should have had someone stay with Boston when the lights went out. He would have complained, but at least he might still be alive.*

I tossed it into the bin and adjusted my shirt. *The engineering suits are almost as well-armored as the defense ones. Metal can't typically get through. Wonder what these creatures are made of.*

I stepped out and turned toward the control room. *Still following step three, Dad. If I fail, I'm sure Sophie will yell at me for you. Looks like they got their suits on. I like the green. The science department definitely has the coolest logos for their fields of study. Sophie's tree in a lab flask looks so cool, and Eliza's got that flask full of crystals with the galaxy sphere on top.* "Got your jumpsuits. Good."

"You should be wearing yours as well," Sophie said, looking over my simple shirt and sweatpants. "You look good in navy blue."

"Got covered in Owen's blood. I'll get another one later. Anyone tell you what happened yet?"

"London stopped by to tell us."

Eliza looks scared. Maybe I should have her keep Owen company for a while. He's good at helping her calm down. "You feeling alright?" I asked.

"I'd feel better if we had more protection," Eliza responded. "Feels vulnerable not having another ship for backup, especially with the issues we've had so far. Why can't we have a defense vessel for our exploration assignments?"

"They try to keep defense ships close to stations for safety. Wouldn't want one wandering around, picking fights."

"Our ship just feels helpless. We do have the shields, but what if we come across something that can get through them?"

"We get the hell out of there," I responded, sitting next to Sophie. "Owen's in his room, taking a break. Hurt his shoulder. Maybe you should keep him company. You know more about medicine than I do, Eliza."

"Yeah, I think I will." She stood and walked out, still holding an uneasy expression.

I closed my eyes and leaned back.

"Maybe you should rest too," Sophie said.

"A nap does sound good. Wake me if something happens."

"Okay."

Chapter 7

"Are you sure we hid them all in here?" Damien asked, rummaging through the cabinet by the fridge.

"Yeah," I said. "That's the one with the weird back panel you can hide things behind."

"We couldn't have gone through all the secret stash already."

"You did tell practically everyone about it."

"Everyone needs a candy bar every now and then. Screw health regulations."

"Find anything?"

"Nope, we're out."

"Not going to get any more from the supply chain," I said.

"We'll have to bring more next time."

Sophie ran in and quickly sealed the door. "They got into the lab."

"You okay?" I asked, walking toward her.

She tightened her grip on the plant in her arms. "Owen was down there with me, he…"

"Is he alive?"

"I'm not sure. The lights went out. He tried getting the lantern back on, but it was dead. He told me to go upstairs.

I grabbed my glowing plant so I could see, then heard him scream…"

"Easy, deep breaths. Did you see anything? Anything that could help us get Owen out?"

"One of the creatures ran up to me. It stopped a few feet away and started shaking its head, keeping its eyes away from my plant, almost like it couldn't handle the glow. I ran up the stairs and Owen…"

"They don't like light. That could work to our advantage." I ran to the other side of the room and grabbed a small blue flashlight. "We can use the prototype inclear lights. It's a self-maintaining power source based on elements we found out in the Embress Galaxy. Once you get it started, it stays powered indefinitely."

Damien grabbed a light. "What if we head down to the lab with these and try to get those things out of the room? Save Owen if he's alive."

"Okay. Sophie, go get the others. Damien and I will close this door behind us. We need someone to watch it."

"Okay. Be careful."

"We will."

Damien slowly opened the door, peering down. "Clear so far."

You'd better be alive… I can't even count how many wild missions you've told me and Damien about. You aren't dying to some alien creatures now.

He stepped down and shifted his light around the room.

63

"Owen?" I whispered. "Where are you?"

The light stopped over a figure lying in the middle of the floor, covered in blood.

No... Owen...

Damien kneeled next to him. "No pulse. Those cuts on his chest are nearly an inch wide."

"How does the door look?"

He stood and turned. "Open. There are scratches on the edge."

"The door closes into the wall. They couldn't have just wedged something into it. Even if it didn't have proper power, the manual lock still should have worked."

"Those two were down here alone?"

"She didn't mention anyone else being here."

"I don't know how they got in unless the door wasn't shut all the way."

"Wait...I hear something."

Gunshots echoed down the hall, followed by rapid footsteps.

"What the hell?" *Who... Hyke! What the fuck is he doing? His gun is broken, and his hand is bleeding.* "Hyke! What the hell are you doing down here?"

"I was checking the door. Heard something messing with it, tearing into the wire panel. I tried to open it a crack to see if I could get a shot. The thing ran down the hall, so I followed."

"You didn't tell anyone or ask for assistance? Sophie and Owen came down after you and got attacked in the lab. Owen's dead."

"What—" His eyes shot over to Owen's body. "I had both of them trapped in the power reserve room. They didn't get by me. How the hell..."

"There must be more than two."

"Is Sophie okay?"

"Yes, she got out fine. We need to seal the door with a block bar. Doubt they would be able to bend pure titanium."

"If they can, I'm activating my emergency pod," Damien said, placing the bar.

Hyke kneeled next to Owen. "What do we do with him? The morgue's in the dark zone."

"We'll have to put him in the medical isolation room for now," I answered. "Get a sample of his blood for analysis and look for any trace of our visitors. We'll need a body bag..." *There's blood everywhere. It's still rushing out over the floor...*

"Why don't you go tell the others?" Damein said, turning me away from Owen's body. "Hyke and I will take care of Owen, then get cleaned up and meet you in the control room."

"Okay..." *Fuck, we lost two people. Should we consider abandoning to the pods? No. We have no power, and the mapping system was acting up before this. We have no way of knowing where those things will try to send us.*

"Owen?" London asked, watching me step into the break room.

"Dead. Grab a body bag from medical."

She nodded and walked out.

"Are you okay?" Sophie asked, stepping closer.

"Only physically. How are you feeling?"

"I'm...not sure."

"Why don't you come to the control room with me? We can sit down while they finish cleaning the lab."

"Okay."

I put my hand on her back and led her through the door. *She's shaking, still holding onto that plant. I know she hasn't been on as many missions, hasn't had to get used to fatalities yet. Sucks how often we lose people out here. Sometimes a whole crew just vanishes... I'm not letting us become one of them.*

We paused in the doorway.

"Control room, sweet control room," I said, looking at his station. It sat to the left of mine, covered in empty coffee cups and a fancy moustache comb. "Won't be the same without him."

"It's going to be quieter," Sophie said, pulling me into my chair.

"Yeah..." My eyes began to water. "He'll be missed."

"I never got to ask him what the flamingoes meant."

I chuckled. "We could really use his smarts to help figure out how to contain these things. Were you able to get a good look at them?"

66

"They're dark, like an oily color with a blue stripe running from behind their black eyes to the edges of their thick, triangular tail. They stand upright. Something moving, waving around on their backs, and a pointed snout. I didn't see a mouth. It's possible they survive primarily on energy. That would explain their ability to drain all three core engines at once."

"Like the plants on V813. They survived off the planet's electrified core. First non-solar-based life we found. That might explain why they didn't like the light. If they're from a planet far from any sun, they wouldn't be used to it."

"Maybe we can use that knowledge to contain them."

"Or we could just shoot them," Hyke said, walking in.

I turned toward him. "I'm not thrilled about the idea of you shooting randomly in the dark."

"The base guns won't do damage to the ship."

"The ones that failed wouldn't, yours will. The one you have in your hand right now. I told you not to bring that thing aboard."

"It's for emergencies. If we need to take down something more powerful—"

"We don't need something that will take us out as well."

"We need—"

"Enough."

Hyke straightened his posture, staring just past me. His face shifted to a serious expression. "I closed the door."

All automatic after practically being raised in the defense department. "Then how did they get through? Those doors seal into the wall."

"I don't know."

"I'm not about to start taking commands from the man that just cost Owen his life. You should have let someone know what you were doing."

"I didn't want to risk anyone else's safety."

"We could have planned a safe procedure. Now we have a broken security door and a dead man. You are to report your location from now on. You will inform someone where you are headed and why, understood?"

His eyes filled with frustration. "Yes, Captain."

Damein stood in the doorway. "We should check the lab camera. See what exactly happened."

"Pull up the footage," I said.

He walked to his station and sat down.

We all got closer, eyes glued to the main screen.

Okay, looks like Hyke was down there for a while, watching the door. He hears something...opens it...starts closing it then runs down the hallway... The door's cracked open... There's Sophie and Owen. Why the hell didn't you check the door, Owen? Two thick claws? Sort of like claws, I guess. They pulled open the door. Sophie and Owen are too busy looking at one of the machines to notice. The lights go out.

"The door wasn't closed all the way." Damien said.

Hyke's eyes flashed with unstable emotion. "I was focused on eliminating the threat, I—"

"You didn't think to secure the door, make sure nothing else was down there with you?"

"Two aliens sneaking onto the ship and not being noticed for days was hard enough to believe."

"You were trained to expect anything. We work on a void exploration vessel, for fuck's sake. We deal with anomalies regularly."

"I..."

"Go take care of your hand."

He turned and walked out, staring down at the floor. His feet shuffled uneasily.

Seen it too many times to count...that sad walk of shame a soldier gets when a comrade is killed. They were taught to save lives.

Sophie stepped closer. "I know he's an ass most of the time, but he didn't mean to."

"I know, but he should have been more careful. Heading straight for a dangerous creature from the void wasn't exactly the smartest idea. The chance that he could have killed one isn't worth the risk to our lives."

"They did kill Boston...and now Owen."

"We don't know why. These are unprecedented creatures. Maybe they wanted to kill them, or maybe there is a misunderstanding. We just don't know enough, and although I loved that man like he was my wild uncle, I'd rather figure out the truth and not rush to conclusions and

69

accidentally start a war with a race we know nothing about."

"You're right. I'm just scared."

"Come sit with me. Everything is okay now. We have block bars up on the side doors and the main door is magnetically sealed into the frame."

She set her plant on Owen's station and sat next to me. "That's still a type of energy."

"Right, but it's still sealed shut into a frame, even if the magnet is drained, we should be okay as long as Hyke doesn't try to play hero again."

"But he loves to play hero."

"He does."

"Those things keep surprising us. We need more information about them. We have no idea how they function; their biology; potential weaknesses."

"What if we do a burst image?" Damien suggested. "Like when the power supply failed on the outer camera and we could only get one snapshot every hour or so. We could program the computer to send a large burst of power to the camera for only a second. Just enough to get the image."

"That might work," I responded.

"I have the commands primed. Thank fuck we have London and Kenneth on electrical." He tapped the screen.

A black and white image of the machine room appeared. One of the creatures stood by the second engine, reaching an arm toward its main control panel.

"That looks freaky," he continued. "What do you think, Sophie?"

"Definitely biological. Muscle mass, eyes, tail. Two legs. Spike-like structures on their backs surrounded by moving tendrils of some sort. One long extended finger-like structure and a long, curled thumb on each hand, though not like any I've seen. Not sure if they can grasp objects."

"That would complicate things. What do we do now, Emma?"

"Monitor the doors and power. Keep everyone out of dark zones."

Sophie leaned into me. "I didn't really expect to find life like this."

"Neither did I," I responded, putting my arm around her. "Most life we've found so far has been simple. Lots of plants. Nothing equal in intelligence to us yet."

"I wonder how intelligent they are."

Damien smiled. "Too bad the comms are broken, or we could ask them. They rushed getting the ship out. Didn't finish the darn things. Owen was able to repair a few of the smaller issues before we left."

"You guys were the first crew selected for this ship?" she asked.

"Yeah, me, Owen, and Emma. We had to get everything ready while they figured out the rest of the crew. It was exciting walking onto a brand-new ship, ready for adventures, then to find out the portside outer camera was faulty, still is, and the comms weren't installed fully."

"Why did they send us out with those problems?"

"The Unitatem Council was pushing for map expansions, and they figured we could finish it ourselves. Didn't realize they forgot to give us the final parts for the comms, and the portside outer camera just has a faulty wire. Can't fix it from the inside."

I gestured toward the screen. "Can we get more pictures?"

Damien pressed a small round button. "I'll send bursts to all the cameras at once so we can get a count. Have any guesses while they're preparing?"

"Three or four. Can't imagine there are any more. Hard to hide a bunch of people-sized creatures."

"Okay, let's see," he said, analyzing the screen. "There's three in the engine room. All other lower rooms are clear."

"They're all looking at the camera," Sophie said.

"That's creepy... I didn't notice that before."

"Could they know it's there? Maybe they feel it. We send an energy burst to take the pictures. Maybe that's why they're all looking at it."

"Makes sense. If they are energy-seeking creatures, they would notice a pulse. Maybe the first one felt the pulse from the first picture, then called the other two over to investigate. Any other observations?"

"I don't think they make any sound, at least that I heard when... Everything was quiet before Owen was attacked."

"I didn't hear any, either," I added.

"These things just keep getting creepier," Damien said. "What do you think we should call them?"

"We don't know enough about their biology to give them a scientific classification," Sophie responded.

"How about corejackers?"

"I like it," I agreed. "They drained our power core."

Sophie smiled and shook her head. "Alright, corejackers. We can come up with their scientific name later once we figure out what they are and where they came from."

This isn't getting better. You have to be quick in the void. If something goes wrong, find it, and get it fixed fast. If you can't, get help. "We need to regain communication."

Damien leaned back. "Even if we manage to get a signal out, we're the only ones who are supposed to be out here. We have to get closer to the map range."

"The only humans who are supposed to be out here," Sophie said. "We've already discovered some type of life in this sector. What if we end up attracting more unidentified life forms with the signal? If something unfriendly responds, we won't be able to defend ourselves in this state."

"We'll wait," I said. "Get ourselves moving, start a signal once we get closer to range."

Damien glanced back at the fuse room. "We'll have to wait until power recharges. Lost too much during Hyke's doomed adventure. Might take a couple days. Ready for suspenseful boredom?"

Chapter 8

"You sure Clarence doesn't have hypnotic abilities?" I asked, walking into the control room.

Sophie was sitting in Owen's chair, staring at the plant on his dashboard. "I'm sure." She smiled and turned toward me. "Just glad I found it. I might not be here if I hadn't."

"Are the others up yet?"

"Eliza and Kenneth are in the lab. She wanted to go over samples again."

"How are you feeling?"

"A little tired. Hard to sleep with what's going on. You?"

I sat next to her. "About the same."

"No matter how much time I spend staring out at the stars, it's still captivating. Especially out here, discovering new space, new galaxies."

"I always wanted to travel though space. Damien and I used to sneak out late at night, lay on the roof, and stare at the sky. He would research the names of stars before going to bed so we could try and find them."

"My uncle is an engineer for Asrocore. He got to take me to work a few times. Told me stories about his trips to space, testing new ships. He helped me get my internship on one of the old Scientific Educational Training vessels."

"My first in space flight training was on one of those S.E.T ships, too. They're supposedly designing new ones."

"Did yours have plumbing problems?"

"Yeah, and the elevators were constantly out of order."

"Not the best ships for your first-time voyage into space."

"They made those back when Owen was in training."

"Which one was he trained on?"

"S.E.T Zero-Zero-Two I think."

"I was on Zero-Two-Four."

"Zero-One-Nine."

"The haunted one?" she asked.

"Supposedly. We could never seem to find who was humming in the hallways at night."

"Humming?"

"Usually started around one AM. I was staying up late with a few friends; heard the humming; went out to look. We followed it for a good half hour. Couldn't find the source."

"Almost wonder if this ship is haunted now. Already had two deaths."

"I'm sure Boston would haunt the engine room. Owen is probably following him around, bugging him with his adventure stories."

"Who or where would you haunt?"

"Damien. I think it would be fun to mess with him."

"You move something. He just stares at it, unphased, and says, 'Really, Emma?'"

"What about you?"

"I'm not sure. I don't think I'd want to haunt my parents. It would be too depressing. I'd probably haunt whatever vessel I died on. Maybe mess with you on weekends." She smiled. "Or if we both die, I'll help you mess with Damien."

"Sounds good. I'd hate to haunt alone."

"Ghosts among the stars."

I looked out the window. The scene was starting to look familiar. Distant stars and planets softly flickered. A deep blue coloration cut through the darkness of the void.

"At least we have a calming view," Sophie said.

"Damien had suggested naming it the cobalt zone."

"Fits well."

I turned back toward the sound of footsteps down the hall. "It's not calming to everyone."

"Is Hyke still frustratedly pacing the hallway?"

"Yup. At least he's alert."

"He keeps insisting on escorting me places."

"You know he likes you."

"He's not the only one." She grinned.

She knows... Well, I haven't been all that subtle. I'm sure London and Damien have been gossiping about me as well.

"He seems a little too eager to fight them," she added.

"His parents were highly respected defense commanders. They raised him to be a soldier. As much of an ass as he is, at least he's prepared."

"Don't they teach soldiers not to have 'relationships' out in space?"

"Yeah, but humankind isn't exactly known for following rules."

"Asrocore does seem pretty relaxed about enforcing them."

"Not exactly easy to enforce rules on a ship, who knows how many miles away, somewhere in space."

"True."

"As long as the same number of people return and nothing is too badly damaged, they're not going to worry about it."

"So we could get away with mischief and no one would know?"

"Pretty much."

Damien walked in. "Gossiping?"

"Talking about Asrocore rules," I explained. "Or lack thereof."

"They're mostly concerned about aliens and deadly diseases. Safety is priority. Social rules are fairly laidback."

Sophie smiled. "Have either of you ever secretly dated anyone on a ship?"

"No," Damien answered, turning to me.

"Neither have I," I said, glaring at him.

"You can get away with it. I can't."

Sophie looked at me. "What?"

"I'm a lesbian. He's straight."

"Asrocore won't do anything about homosexual couples," Damien explained. "Less risk of accidental children."

Sophie smiled. "Guess I just have to stick with women, then."

Damien sighed. "I'm probably going to be single for a while."

I smirked at him. "Sucks to be straight."

Two small beeps grabbed at our attention.

Damien rushed to his station and sat down. "Security footage was successfully restored."

I walked toward him. "See if you can pull up the last camera footage before the power drained."

"Which section?"

"Check the engine room first. See if anything strange shows up before the power went out. We can also confirm everyone's locations when it did."

"Looks like Boston was next to the first engine, drinking coffee, grumbling to himself about something, as usual. The room was humming with energy, clean and well-maintained, nothing out of the ordinary. Boston's looking up at the ceiling, watching the lights fade...then he swears, and the room goes dark. Camera shuts off. That's it. I don't see anything. Not a single out of place shape, not even a suspicious shadow."

"There are too many blind spots. They could have been hiding in any one of the lower-level rooms."

"Think they're smart enough to know to avoid the cameras?"

"They didn't just waltz through the ship."

"Maybe they can be invisible...wait, here." Damien pointed to the screen. "Five minutes before we lost power. Cameras B4, B2, B5, then B6 all go off for a few seconds."

"Any idea why?"

"No, but it is weird... They seem to go off in a specific order, from the storage room, to the hallway, then through the security door into the next hallway, then into the oxygen room."

Sophie stepped closer. "Almost like something moved between the rooms."

"The oxygen camera continues to flicker afterward, and it looks like that room stayed at slightly lower power."

"Where is everyone at this time?" I asked.

"Looks like Sophie and Eliza were sitting in the lab going over samples, Owen was asleep, Boston was by the engines, Kenneth and Hyke were in the gym, and you and London were helping me out of my room."

"No one was in that section. Do all the cameras go off at once after that?"

"The oxygen cam goes off first, just before the rest."

"Maybe they can control how much they drain," Sophie suggested. "If they just drained everything constantly, the power wouldn't have turned back on in the rooms they walked through. It would make sense why we didn't notice anything on board until now. They could have just hid and waited."

"Perspicacious creatures," Damien said.

"What?" Sophie asked.

"Fancy word for intelligent. So how do we contain this problem safely?"

"I'm not sure. We don't know anything about them aside from their ability to drain energy, mechanical or biological. Anything that has energy will be..." She stopped and looked back at the door.

"What?"

"The algae tanks. They might have been drained as well. It's in the dark zone. Even if we get the lights back on soon, the algae system is probably done."

"Then we only have oxygen reserves?"

"Until we get power back on. The garden plants might help, if they're still alive, but they aren't enough to sustain the whole ship with oxygen."

"How much oxygen can those fancy space rocks produce without the algae?"

"Not enough."

"So, we've been invaded by deadly creatures who have most likely killed off our oxygen and food supplies. Great. Would be nice if we could discover some type of alien detecting rock. Alerts us when aliens sneak on board. It could exist. You never know."

Sophie sighed. "Why couldn't we find a nice, calm species? Space bunnies, butterflies."

"Cats," I said with a chuckle. "It has put a damper on discovering new life. Find something cool that immediately wants to kill you. That's what happens in all the old space movies."

"At least we try to be peaceful first. That's why research companies like Asrocore and Exploration Frontier are allowed full space access."

"Could you imagine what it would be like if Void Defense ran us?"

"We'd be taking orders from Hyke. Yikes. That would suck."

"Regulations would be far stricter. Every ship would have an exterior weapons system."

"That wouldn't be too bad. We do have the shield barrier, but not having outer weapons does make me a little uneasy at times, especially knowing literally anything could be out there."

"Space is strange."

Chapter 9

I looked down at my tablet. The screen flashed. *Connection error. I'm starting to get used to our constant problems.*

London walked in and handed me a coffee mug. "Same?"

"Yup."

Damien sat in front of his desk, messing with wires. "Didn't bring me one?"

"Not when you're working on electronics," she said. "How are we doing on power?"

"Forty-four percent. Still can't move until we get one of the engines up and running. All motion depends on those. We don't have either of our mechanic experts or access to the cores. At least we're still following step three."

"For now."

"If we do die, you and Kenneth are welcome to make our condolence video for our dad."

She grinned. "What, you don't want Hyke to do it?"

"Fuck no. That man only knows how to speak defense technique, fluent arguer, and shitty flirting."

"Who've you heard him flirting with?"

"Sophie. Mostly when we first got assigned. She didn't seem very interested, and he eventually backed off. Guess it's your chance now, Emma. You seem more her type. Want some advice?"

I turned toward him. "From you?"

"I was once a hopeless romantic."

"You dated one girl in college."

"Space is a daring adventure no matter where you're going. We rely on those around us to survive. We appreciate more, accepting limitations for the cost of an adventure. The bonds you make millions of miles from home are fiercely strong. If you have strong feelings for her, go for it. Sure, rejection is far worse out in space, since you can't leave, but I doubt she would say no."

"I'm sure Owen is berating you in the afterlife for stealing one of his motivational quotes."

"I think I do a pretty good job. His words should be told by someone just as talented and good looking."

"Are you complimenting him or calling yourself old?"

"He might look young again as a ghost."

"Shut up and keep following step three." *Looks like Sophie's walking in. She's got that wild idea look in her eye. Much prettier on her than Damien. When he does it you know he's about to say or do something ridiculous.*

Sophie stopped in front of me, holding a beaker of luminescent liquid. "Emma, remember the story you told me about Owen's chemist friend that made herself glow?"

"Yeah... Oh, yeah, good idea. We have enough power now to look up the ingredients."

Damien stole my mug and took a sip. "So, let me get this straight, we're making soap so we glow in the dark to not get eaten by aliens?"

"Pretty much."

"Great story for Dad."

I looked at Sophie. "Need any help?"

"Can you bring the large, full body soap jug from storage down to the lab? I'll get the rest of the chemicals and meet you at my desk." She turned and eagerly walked out.

Damien grinned at me. "Have fun doing science with your future girlfriend."

I grabbed the mug from his hand. "Taking this habit from Owen as well?"

"You were too focused on her to notice."

"Fair, but I'm taking it with me."

You'd better not encourage him to take any more of your traits from beyond the grave, old man. Let's see, down the hall, through the door, down the next hall, and to the left. Glad we actually keep this room clean and organized. For the shit we've had to deal with, we got an efficient crew.

"You can't efficient your way out of death, Emma. Arther knew that."

"But if we—"

"Shush. No more. We all could have been the most efficient workers in the universe and he still would have died. Things go wrong, no matter how right we all are."

I closed my eyes. "You were right, Owen. Still hurts. My best friend, my crewmates, you...her... On earth or here. In the middle of a roaring thunderstorm or the silence of a void. Death still hurts."

I opened my eyes and walked along the shelves of supplies. *Soap, soap, soap. Got it. One large jug should do. Back into the hallway, back up the hall, third door to the right, through the break room, down the stairs into lab two, and set this on the pretty blonde's desk.*

"Perfect," Sophie said, messing with chemical vials.

Eliza turned towards me. "Never thought I'd be going back to college pranks for void safety, but I have to admit, I love the charm."

"I'm sure some of the wilder college students would win fights with our creatures on pure caffeine and spite alone," I said. "Sometimes you need some drunk at two in the morning ideas to get through difficult situations."

"Just have to be careful in knowing which of those ideas will save your life, and which will get you expelled."

"Always go for the middle ground professors. Damien and his friends had a list of the ones who were cool and laid back, the ones who were quiet and just did their jobs, and the ones who complained about every little thing. His statistics major friend said the ones who aren't too calm but also won't explode with rage were the ones to go for. They might laugh it off or get upset, but they weren't going to march to the principal and demand anything serious."

"Really? My friends also had a list like that, though theirs was simpler, only two categories."

Sophie reached out. "Pause for a second and get me the—"

Eliza picked up a small brown bottle from her desk and handed it to her.

"Yes, that, perfect."

"She didn't even say anything," I said.

"It's not a difficult thing to make," Eliza responded. "I can tell what she needs by what she already has on her desk."

"How many times did you make things like this in college?"

"A few times for my close friends. I was never directly in on the action, though."

"Prefer to be the chemical mastermind behind the scenes?"

"I charged people in snacks."

"Great profit."

Sophie paused and turned toward us. "I forgot we don't have working showers…"

"We can make a jumpsuit dye instead," Eliza recommended.

"Perfect!"

"Hold on." She stood and placed a hand on Sophie's shoulder. "I'll finish this. You've been up for too long. You should get some rest."

"But—"

She pulled Sophie toward me and looped our arms together. "Take her to her room, Emma."

I nodded. "Okay."

"No more science until you've had a proper eight hours."

Sophie followed me up the stairs. "Fine."

"When did you get up this morning?" I asked.

"Three."

"Yeah, you should get some sleep."

"It's been hard lately with everything going on. I don't want to be alone right now."

I stopped in the hallway. "I can stay with you, get cozy and relax."

"Sure."

"Hot chocolate and a movie?"

"Do we have enough power for that?"

"The tablets don't take much. My room okay? I want to be close to control just in case."

"Sure."

I opened my bedroom door. *Alright, time for ultimate coziness and relaxation. Not easy in a small room with death one floor down, but I'll do my best.* I led her to my bed and wrapped a fuzzy blanket around her.

"What movie?" she asked, getting out her tablet.

"You pick while I grab the hot chocolate."

I stepped out, leaving the door open. *We should still have some. Luckily Owen wasn't as fond of stealing that. Let's see...kitchen, upper right cabinet, behind the weird electrolyte drinks. Looks like four packs left. Should be more in storage. Just have to flash the water, mix the powder. I'll use the kitten mugs. There, perfect. Too bad Damien ate all the marshmallows. I wonder what she picked.*

I walked back into my room and sat next to her, handing her a mug. "Alright, the coziness and beverages are done, what entertainment are we getting?"

"*Follies of the Ocean King.*"

"Haven't seen that one before."

"It started as a dramatic opera in the 1900s. Made into a movie in the early 2000s, then a hologram opera a few years ago."

"What's it about?"

"A lonely king meets a siren after his son dies at sea."

"What version are we watching tonight?"

"I was thinking of starting with a recording of the oldest version. Phonographs and black and white cameras. I thought it would help get my mind off all the high-tech danger we're currently dealing with. Sometimes I like to think about simpler times, read old books, and just think about what life would be like. Wake up with the sun and walk through a garden of colorful flowers. No need to worry about oxygen, or void-based life forms. Just flowers and animals."

"What sort of animals?"

"I like birds. My mother goes birdwatching with her sisters every Thursday. She used to take me with her when I was little."

"Favorite bird?"

"A partial albino stellar jay. I saw one for the first time when my mother took me on a trip to the Skybrook Wells Nature Reserve. I was...six, I think. We had to get up early and walk for a while. My aunt carried me most of the way. They stopped at this beautiful park and found a bench next to a small tree. I was tired and unamused until my mom told me to look up. There were birds soaring through the sky, carefree. The sun had just begun to rise, making all their feathers shine. I was confused when I saw what looked like a half a bird flying around. It landed on the tree next to us. Most of its right side and tail had normal bright blue feathers, but its left side, chest, and head were completely white with dapples of grey in between. My aunt drew a picture of me staring at it."

"Not an early morning kid, huh?"

"No." She activated her tablet and showed me the screen. The background was a pencil drawn image of a small, wavy-haired child staring wide-eyed at a bird in a small tree.

Little Sophie is adorable. Her hair hasn't changed a bit. "Cute. Does she always draw the birds?"

"Yes. She would bring her fancy colored pencils everywhere with her."

"Bet it wasn't the easiest task."

"You'd think so, but my aunt either has incredibly good luck or can talk to animals. Whatever birds she starts drawing always stays still for most of the process."

"Lucky indeed."

"One of the park guides came by and told us facts about the birds. Apparently the one I was staring at was one of their rarest. Most partial albino jays' colors divide front to back with white heads and speckles running down their bodies, not one side white and one blue. That bird's name was Opal. My mom and aunts started taking me there every year on my birthday to see her. I even got to hold her a few times."

"Surprised you didn't become an ornithologist."

"I did, but there aren't exactly birds out here, so I also got a degree in botany."

"Then I assume you know plenty about sleepless study nights."

"Too much. What about you? What animal is your favorite?"

"Spectacled bear. They look like they're either wearing war paint, funny goggles, or they're pretending to be a racoon."

She chuckled and leaned her head against my shoulder. "They do."

"Getting tired?"

"A little."

"Still want to watch the opera?"

"Yes." She reached forward and placed her tablet on the table.

"I haven't watched an opera in... I don't actually remember when. I'm sure Dad had us watch one at some point."

She leaned back against me and pulled the blanket over us.

Watching a 1900s, black and white opera while sitting in one of the most advanced void ships out in unexplored galaxies...oddly calming.

Sophie smiled. "I bet Owen would sing along if he was here."

I laughed. "I'm sure he'd impress us by knowing every song in the show."

Chapter 10

Damien, control room. Owen...morgue. Sophie is with me. Eliza, London, Kenneth, all in the kitchen. Hyke, breakroom. Boston, morgue.

Damien walked into the hallway. "Morning, you two. Spend the night together?"

Sophie smiled. "We were watching an opera. I fell asleep."

"Safety in numbers."

"Status?" I asked him.

"Fifty percent power. Doors are still secure. Eliza finished the dye, we're just waiting for its chemicals to 'settle' before we apply them to our suits. Breakfast is in the cafeteria."

"What is it?"

"Eggs and toast."

"Sounds good."

"Can you two grab us some more pepper from the kitchen?"

"Sure."

Sophie followed me down the hall. "Which cabinet is it in?"

"Over by the oven."

"We're going to run out again if London keeps dumping it on her food."

"Kenneth said she's been doing that since she was little. The moment she was introduced to pepper, she started putting it on everything."

"Everything?"

"Did he tell you about the time she tried to cook a Christmas turkey dinner?"

"No."

"She apparently put so much pepper on it that it looked charred."

"Really?"

"Only true daredevils ate turkey that night."

"I wonder if—" She stopped and stared at the ceiling.

The lights slowly faded. A dim blue glow filled the room.

Fuck, not again. "Sophie, do you still have your inclear light?"

"I set it down to grab the pepper..."

"The stairway door just opened."

"The one in here?"

"Yes." *Wait...something's moving by the window. A dark silhouette against the stars. Upright figure, pointed snout, something waving around above its back.* "Sophie," I whispered, reaching for her.

The figure charged forward, knocking me down. Its claws tore into my leg. *Ahh! Where the hell is the light... Fuck!* "Sophie, get out!"

It placed a foot onto my injured leg and leaned closer.

Dear Dad, I'm an idiot. I should have kept the gun with me after London fixed it.

"I found it!" she yelled, shining it toward the creature.

Damn that thing looks weird. Oily color. No wonder it blends into the shadows so well. Definitely hates that light... It's running back down the stairs.

"You okay?" Sophie asked, shutting the door.

"I'll be fine."

She grabbed the med kit and kneeled next to me. "Let me take a look."

Damien ran in. "What happened?"

"One got up here," I responded.

"Where is it now?"

"It ran back into lab one."

Sophie gently shifted my leg. "It looks deep. You're going to need stitches to stop the bleeding."

"Think you can handle it?"

"I'll try."

Damien looked at me. "You okay with that?"

"She's got two degrees in biology. That's good enough for me. Just make sure someone keeps an eye on that door."

"Got it." He picked me up and stepped out of the room. "Kenneth, Hyke, get a block bar on the kitchen door and check all dark zone access doors!" he yelled.

Hyke rushed into the hall. "On it."

Damien carried me to the medical room and set me down on the table.

Sophie ran to the counter and grabbed a syringe from one of the drawers and injected it into my leg.

"What's that?" I asked.

"A numbing agent. Try to stay still."

Damien sat next to me, holding my hand.

The pain faded. I stared at the blood dripping onto the table. Everything began to blur. Flashes of thunder; rain falling to the ground. *The tree...*

"Emma?" Damien moved his other hand to my shoulder.

"I'm okay."

"We're going to need to be more careful. We can't afford to lose anyone else."

"Almost done," Sophie said, carefully tying the sutures. "You might have trouble moving it for a while. I'll wrap it up. Stay off it for at least a day. I'd prefer longer, but I know you won't want to cooperate."

Damien glared at me. "Never does."

Sophie sat next to me. "Did Hyke go on another hero adventure?"

"No," Damien responded. "Kenneth, Hyke, and I took turns keeping watch last night. Hyke didn't leave the main hallway. No one went down there this morning, either. Everyone had just gotten up. I'll go check the cameras."

Sophie looked out the window. Her hand was shaking.

I gently grabbed it. "Hey, you okay, Sophie?"

"They keep getting through the doors. We don't have anywhere to go. We...might actually die."

I put my arm around her. "It's possible, but we probably won't."

She smiled. "You sound like Owen."

"The control room is set up with emergency supplies: water, food, medical equipment. The door has a special Kethon-based lock. If anything happens, we'll be safe there. Asrocore will send someone to find us if we're out of range for too long. They might even already know something's wrong if the supply ship is down as well."

"We don't really have any other options, do we? Even if the corejackers stay downstairs, oxygen's not going to last forever..."

"At least we'd have an interesting death."

She smiled. "What if we can't leave the ship as ghosts? I don't exactly want to be stuck with Hyke."

"We can throw him out of the airlock. I'm not haunting this ship with him forever."

"I'm sure everyone would agree to that."

"Heck, maybe we should just throw him out now, see if the corejackers follow him."

She laughed. "Slow motion space chase."

"I wonder if they can move through the void on their own. They could be capable of anything, for all we know. At least they wouldn't be able to get near Earth. Doubt they would go anywhere near a sun."

"I wonder how many aliens we haven't seen because of the conditions of our solar system. There could be an entire ecosystem of creatures like them, and we would never have known if we never left."

"There could be another intelligent race out there that might just not be able to survive in our natural habitat."

"Probably a good thing. People already suck at managing invasive species on Earth. I don't think we would do well against an invading alien species."

"The Incipience Safety Core should be able to hold them back. That's what they're trained for, at least."

"True."

Damien walked back in with a troubled expression. "Emma...you need to see this." He handed me his tablet.

Okay, footage of lab one. Looks fine... Wait, the error lights are flashing. The door opened... One shadow rushed in...then the lights went out. "At least it was only one. How did they get it open?"

"Hyke said he heard them messing with the lab two door before Owen was attacked. Maybe they damaged this one as well."

"Fuck... I was too distracted by Owen's death to listen to Hyke's concerns. The entire reason he opened the lab two door in the first place. I should have thought about blocking the lab one door sooner..."

"We didn't know they could get through the properly functioning doors. Especially with how hard they are to open manually. Thay would have had to cut the power, then learn how to use the seal bar and press the release button."

"That's concerning." Sophie said, scooting closer.

"Did they know it was a door?" I asked.

"They have been moving around the ship for a while," Damien responded. "Maybe they learned how to open them, or they learned our door mechanics from the supply ship."

"Well, the main stairwell has a double door with a magnetic lock. It has extra protection in case something goes wrong with the cores. They shouldn't be able to get through there."

"We said that before. These things love to surprise us. We're going to run out of ship eventually. I'm almost tempted to just sic Hyke on them. The man's stubborn enough. He'll probably be able to eliminate them all and survive."

"And blow us up in the process. Do you think they're immune to energy blast explosions considering they seem to absorb it?"

"Possibly," Sophie responded. "Depends on how exactly they absorb energy and how much they can absorb at once. They are biologically based life forms. Everything has limits."

"So..." Damien started. "We might be dealing with creatures that wouldn't even blink at C4? Great! At least we have a really, really good excuse why we didn't follow step three. Dear Dad, sorry we died, but we couldn't really help it when we encountered explosion-proof aliens."

I smiled. "He'd understand."

London excitedly rushed in. "We have an idea. We cut off all power connections to the lab one observation room, take everything out, shut off all surrounding power, place a decoy inside connected to a power source, and see if we can trap them. Kenneth can set up one of our smaller solar batteries in the room next to it. I can program it to occasionally give them an energy burst in case they need it to survive. They would be contained, and we could still study them."

"We would have to clear the lab first. We've already lost two crew. Opening any of those doors would be a risk."

"If there's a chance to capture them, I think we should take it."

"We don't even know if any of the lab one equipment has taken damage. There still might be a corejacker in there."

"We can always try to do a burst image so we can see if the lab is empty."

"They're drawn to energy; they might head straight for the lab if we do that."

"True..."

"Send a burst to the engine room," I suggested. "That should lure them there so we can clear the lab safely. How long will it take to set up the room?"

"A day at least, maybe two. We'll need to disconnect all wires."

"Alright, do it. Make sure the door seals properly. Don't let Hyke anywhere near it."

"Got it." She walked out.

"I should go to control and—"

Sophie put a hand on my shoulder. "No walking, remember?"

"Okay, just wish I could help them."

Damien stood up. "I've got an idea. I'll be right back."

Sounds chaotic out there. Everyone rushing around getting ready to clear the room. Hyke sounds excited, not surprising. Kenneth is nervous. London is teasing him about it. There are voices missing... Owen, Boston... I know Owen would be encouraging Kenneth right now, telling him a story to help lighten the mood. Boston would be constantly complaining about not being able to have access to the engines. I should have known something was wrong.

Damien walked back in, handing me his tablet. "I put a camera on Hyke. Now we can watch." He sat next to me.

"You chose the action adventure rout?" I said.

"Would you have preferred I put it on Kenneth?"

"No, Hyke is more reactive. We'll see more of the situation from his perspective."

"Then shush and watch."

The room went quiet.

I really hope things go well. I'd prefer not to have us watch another crew member die...

"Ready?" Hyke asked.

"Ready," Kenneth responded.

They stood in the kitchen next to the stairway door.

Hyke opened it slowly, flashing the inclear light down the stairs. "Clear," he said, walking down.

Nothing looks out of place so far. At least they don't trash every room they enter. I'd almost prefer it if they would. That'd make finding them much easier.

"Movement by the hall door," Kenneth said.

Hyke turned. "I don't see it. Must have been scared off. The room looks clear." He cautiously stepped toward the hallway and peeked around the corner. "They shredded the door panel."

"We'll have to bar it."

Hyke stepped back in and kept a light on the door.

Kenneth placed the bar. "At least they don't eat so they don't produce waste. Would suck to have to clean up alien shit."

"More or less than having to work in the eco-waste sector?"

"I don't know. Depends on which smells worse."

"Maybe we'll figure that out during our next alien encounter."

"With our luck we'll end up encountering all the unfriendly ones. Bet I'll outlive you."

"Your scrawny tech-loving ass?"

"I can at least tech my way out of most bad situations. You just want to shoot everything."

Damien smiled. "He's not wrong."

I set down the tablet. "Surprisingly uneventful. Hope their plan works."

Chapter 11

Hyke stood unnervingly still, staring at the door.

Wonder how long he's been there...how paranoid he's going to be about the doors from now on. Maybe I should talk to him when we get out of this situation. I know what it's like to fear something so simple...a door, the rain... I've never seen him this paranoid. "Hyke?"

"Haven't heard anything," he responded. "No sign that they've tried getting in yet."

"If you need to take a break, Damien or I can take over."

"It's fine. You'll be needed to get this thing moving again."

"Alright." I turned toward the long-haired man hunched over in the observation room, messing with wires.

"Why don't we ever use this lab?" Kenneth asked, looking up at Sophie. "Everything seems to be working."

She handed him a small tool. "Eliza doesn't like to be alone for very long, so we always used two."

"I get it. It's more fun to chat with London while we work. Being alone would be boring."

"Eliza gets nervous. I guess she grew up with several siblings. Being alone just isn't normal for her."

"Did any of them end up working in space as well?"

"One of her brothers works on a base closer to Earth. I think the rest of them are still home. They run some sort of animal rescue, I think."

"How's it going in there?" I asked.

Kenneth held up a simple radio. "We'll use this to lure them in. I spent all of yesterday getting the main power connections disconnected. This radio will be the only energy source. I have it wired to the same burst system that the cameras are on. We can control it from upstairs without it risking our power. I also set up an extra camera in here so we can keep an eye on our captives."

"What about the door?"

"Just needed a quick function test. These observation doors are already set up to seal things in."

"What's the plan?"

"London made a timer lock for the main lab door. Once the room is ready, I'll start the timer so we can get out and shut off power to this room before opening the door."

"How much longer?"

"Maybe twenty minutes or so. We still have to finish the radio and do a final test."

"Anything I can help with?"

"Go to the control room and see if you get a feed on the new camera. It should be titled OBSER1."

"Got it."

Sophie followed me to the stairs. "Hold on, you'll need help. I don't want you straining that leg."

"I got down here just fine."

"Don't argue. Give me your arm. You shouldn't be climbing stairs right now."

"It doesn't hurt, just feels weak."

"Let me help you anyways."

"Such a sweetheart."

"Would you rather have Damien carry you around more?"

"Not particularly."

Her eyes shifted into every room as we made our way down the hall. "If only the wheelchairs didn't get stuck in the dark zone. Why weren't they in med bay?"

"Kenneth and Damien were jousting with them in the lower hallway."

"What's a good word for goof-offs?"

"Rabble-rousers, firebrands, or stirrers."

"I like rabble-rousers," she said, glaring at Damien as we stepped into control.

He turned toward us. "Fantastic word choice."

"It fits you and Kenneth well."

London stepped closer and nodded. "I agree."

"Any particular reason for this sudden vocabulary joust?" Damien asked.

Sophie crossed her arms. "Your wheelchair jousting."

"Ah, yeah those would be useful right about now..."

London sat in Owen's chair. "Next time, we're leaving you trapped in your room."

"Alone? That would go against our buddy system." He smiled at me. "A plus for following the rules."

"Emma didn't go down there with a buddy."

"But she came back with one."

"Those two have been practically glued to each other since she got hurt," London added.

"And you've been hanging around me a lot. People might get suspicious."

She threw a cat plush at him. "Would you rather Hyke keep you company?"

"He'd just stare at the door or pace the whole time."

I picked up the other plush and threw it at him. "Stop jabbering. Kenneth wants us to try the observation room camera. Should be titled OBSER1."

He turned and tapped on his screen. "OBSER1, connected and clear."

London stood. "We'll have to go down to tell him. His tablet won't be able to get a signal down in that room with all the energy blockades we've put up. Sophie and I can go. Damien will be needed for the cameras, and you, Emma" —she placed her hands on my shoulders and sat me in my chair— "need to sit down, give that leg a rest."

"We'll be right back," Sophie said, following her out.

Damein turned toward me and smirked. "How's it going?"

"What?"

"You two have been staying close. Haven't asked her out yet?"

"While we're struggling for survival against deadly aliens? Not exactly the best time."

"Fair enough. You think this will work?"

"Kenneth once told me how they caught a crazed squirrel using only a tree branch and a car battery."

"How the hell did they do that?"

"No idea, but it definitely makes me breathe easier knowing those two are on it."

"Hyke still staring at the door?"

"Barely blinks," I answered.

"He hasn't been sleeping well. Still shaken about Owen's death."

"We all are."

"I know he can be an ass, but he's never been a hazard to anyone. He's all about safety and protecting innocent lives. This kind of screw-up really digs into that kind of mentality. Especially with how he was raised."

"His parents probably won't treat him well once they hear. They aren't big fans of failure."

"Pernickety people."

"Not quite, more...overscrupulous."

"With a dash of vaunting."

I smiled. "Maybe we should make him read the dictionary. It would be a nice distraction and help him understand our insults about his parents."

"Dad would be proud."

"Until we died because our fancy speech has no effect on non-English speaking aliens."

"Dear Dad, we all died, but did it with a wondrously sophisticated vocabulary."

"Maybe Owen should have tried lecturing the alien to death."

"Maybe."

Fuck, I don't even want to imagine how bad Hyke will feel if people back home learn about how Owen died. People loved that energetic old man. Hyke never had as good a reputation. It was an accident, but people on Earth especially get nosey and accusatory, faulting mistakes. It will be reported, but I can keep quiet about exactly how the door failed. Even he doesn't deserve to be hounded after all this... Fuck, why are the lights dimming again?

Damien grabbed Owen's gun and walked toward the door, shining its light down the hall. "That's not supposed to happen."

"Could they have gotten up here somehow?" I asked, following close behind.

"I don't know. The doors were all sealed, unless Hyke went for another catastrophe adventure. Was anyone still up here?"

"Eliza was in her room. Everyone else is in lab one."

She opened her door, walking toward us. "What's going on?"

"We're not sure," Damien answered. "Stay with us for now."

"Okay."

"We should try to put up our defense at the end of the personnel hallway. Then we'd still have the pods."

"Were you able to finish the mapping repair?" I asked.

"Not entirely."

"Those pods won't be able to get us back to base with partial maps. Either we risk floating off into uncharted space, hoping to get found before we perish, or we make a stand here. The emergency door between personnel and the rest of the ship is the same as the lab doors, they'll just get through again. The control room door has bolt locks; it's our best bet at safety."

"Okay."

"We need to get everyone up here."

"We have to be careful. We don't know where the corejackers are."

"Did you see anything on the cameras?"

"No, though I was primarily focusing on the new one the last few minutes."

"Whatever happens, we can't let them get into the control room."

"Got it."

Gunshots echoed from the kitchen.

Kenneth burst through the door and ran toward us. "The light!"

Damien turned it toward the large, shadowed mass behind him.

It turned suddenly, fumbling into the wall before darting into the break room.

"You okay?" I asked, turning back.

"Yeah," Kenneth answered, catching his breath.

"Where are the others?"

"Downstairs. I'm not sure how the creatures got in."

"Damien, keep that light on the break room door."

"Got it."

I rushed to the emergency panel and pulled out a small handgun. *This one's heat based, I believe. Hopefully that works.*

"What are you—"

"Do not let them into this room," I said, dashing down the hall.

"Emma!"

I can hear more gunshots coming from lab one. Hopefully everyone is in there and alive. I stepped into the stairwell. Glowing blue liquid dripped down the dark grey wall, covering the middle steps. *Blaster gun marks. Looks like someone shot the tube... Hyke's in the corner, gun facing the door. London's behind him. Her side is bleeding.*

"Where's Sophie?" I whispered.

London walked toward me. "I don't know. The lights shut off. One came from the kitchen stairs, then two more were pulling the hallway door open. Everyone panicked. Have you seen Kenneth?"

"He made it to the control room. Damien and Eliza are with him. The creature that chased him is hiding in the break room. You said one came down the stairs first?"

"Yes."

"How the hell did they get there? The main stairwell door was still secure."

"I don't know. Hyke shot one of the bio panels to see if the fluid would stop it. Confused it for a second but didn't seem to do any damage."

"You need medical treatment. Hyke, take her up, then come back to me. I'll make sure the other two don't get past."

"On it." He took her arm and helped her up the stairs.

Be quick. We need to find Sophie. Come on... Come on... Please be okay. I can't look for you by myself. Not when there's two. Come on, Hyke. I'm fighting every logical fiber in my body not to just run out to find her. She's smart and she has a light, I'm sure she's fine. Please be fine...

"Ready?" Hyke asked, rushing back down the stairs.

"You look left, I'll look right."

"Roger."

We quickly turned around the corners, lighting the hallway.

"Blood trail to the right," I said. "No movement."

"Clear to the left. I'll follow."

Why the hell is it so quiet? Are they intentionally being silent or do they just not make sound? Come on, Sophie, where are you?

"In here," Hyke said, stopping by the armory door.

A bright light flashed into our eyes. "Sorry!" Sophie whispered.

She grabbed a gun, good. "You okay?" I asked.

She ran up and hugged me. "Just a scratch. You?"

"I'm fine. Did you see where they went?"

"They chased me in here, then darted off toward the lab."

"We didn't see them. They must have passed it."

"We need to get back to the others," Hyke said, stepping toward the door.

"I'll lead. You keep an eye behind us."

"Roger."

I slowly stepped toward the door, peering around the corners. *No movement so far. Looks like I left glowing footprints behind. That's handy. A nice little glowing trail to lead us back. Sophie and Hyke are following. I don't see anything in the lab. Better check the corners just in case... It's clear. Stairs are still dripping blue. Kitchen is empty. They're both still with me. Step three... Step three...*

A flash of gunfire erupted behind me. Hyke fell back against the wall.

The corejacker lunged forward, trying to knock his weapon out of his hand.

Fuck, this one's getting bold. I grabbed one of the chairs, throwing it at the creature's head. "Run to control!"

Hyke pushed it off, following behind. Another creature jumped out at us from the break room.

"Quick!" Damien yelled.

Sophie ran ahead.

My head rang with every flash of light, every shot, every step. I could feel my heart pounding, every inch of my body tensed up, hoping nothing was about to tear into me.

Damien grabbed my hand, helping me slow down. "Where's Hyke?"

"He was just behind me..." I turned back. The hallway was empty and quiet. "Where the fuck did they go?"

"We only saw you and Sophie come through the hallway door."

"Is he still in the kitchen? We got the creature off of him."

"Wait," London said, shining a light down the hall.

Two shadows lingered by the kitchen door.

"We can't fight them like this," I said, checking my weapon. "One of them ran right for Hyke even with the lights on it. They're getting desperate. We have to shut the door."

"Hyke's still out there," Kenneth said.

"With three creatures that don't seem to give a damn about our guns! This door is our only point of safety."

Sophie grabbed my arm. "They're running toward us!"

"Shut it!" I repeated.

A loud thud, then all went silent.

Sophie sat next to me, shaking.

I put my arm around her and whispered. "We'll be fine, I promise." I looked back at Kenneth. "Is the radio functional?"

He glanced down at his tablet. "Almost."

"Activate it as soon as you can."

"If Hyke is still alive they might not all go for it. What do we do? We can't just leave him out there with them."

113

"Half of us are injured. Our bullets don't seem to be doing anything to them. We cannot risk opening that door until they are contained."

"There's...nothing we can do for him?"

"We can help him after they're trapped."

"If he lives. Those things don't exactly fool around."

"Hyke's been through every resilience course imaginable. If anyone's going to survive those things, it's him."

Gunshots rang out from behind the door. Kenneth jumped back. Sophie grabbed onto me. London got out a knife.

Come on, Hyke, get them. For Owen...

Silence filled the room, reminding me of who we had lost. *It was quiet for them too... Every time things went wrong... I never realized how consuming the uncertainty of silence could be.*

Damien leaned against the door. "Hyke... Hyke, knock if you can hear me."

Silence responded. Not a single breath or footstep. No hums from the ship, no video game sounds, crinkling snack bags, no words, no stories, as if the ship itself were a void.

I glanced over at the glowing plant still sitting on Owen's station. *We could really use some of your optimism right now, old man.*

"Radio's on," Kenneth said. "Sending a burst to the camera." He tapped the screen. "They're following it. Two

114

are in...three! Door's closed. All are in. Power should return in a few minutes."

"Open the door," I said. "Sophie, London, and Eliza, stay here."

"You sure you're up for this, Emma?" Damien asked.

"I'll be fine." *I'm not accepting any more fatalities.*

He tapped the panel and opened the door.

We stood in the quiet for a few moments, watching the lights slowly flicker back on.

Hyke, you asshole, you'd better be alive...

Damien stepped out, following a thick trail of blood. "Think he's alive?"

"Might be, just to spite them," I said, following close behind.

Kenneth stopped at the storage room door. "Hyke?"

I froze, my eyes affixed to the dark red puddle in the doorway. Oily splotches mixed into it. The pain in my leg screamed for my attention. Thunder and rain thrashed around in my head. *My leg... The tree... The blood...*

"Hey." Damien nudged my shoulder.

I shook my head, looking up at him. "I'm okay."

Kenneth shined his light into the room and let out a sigh. "He didn't make it."

"We'll get his body in the morgue as soon as we secure the rest of the ship."

"I'll lead," Damien offered, stepping ahead of me.

He always notices when it gets to me. Focus, Emma. *Time to head down the hall, into the main stairwell. The walls and ceiling are riddled with bullet holes. There's blood splattered on the third engine. My glowing footprints... My head is starting to hurt.* "Clear the floor first, then we can activate the engines," I said, turning down the hallway.

Kenneth ran into lab one and walked up to one of the observation computers. "Infra-red camera is working. Three creepy corejackers all trapped. One's sitting against the door, looks badly injured. Door is secure, they aren't getting out."

"We've said that before."

"The observation glass in front of us is Coretech space certified, bullet proof, explosion proof, fireproof, freezeproof, and every other kind of indestructible you can imagine. The walls are reinforced, four inches thick. They made these observation rooms to contain all possible anomalies we might find out here. With the added power cutting and the unreasonable amount of rubber covering I placed over the remaining wires in the wall, nothing is getting out of there."

"Okay, okay, you win."

"Damien and I can check the rest of the rooms, just in case. Once we're done, we'll stay down here to keep an eye on our captives. You should head back upstairs and let the others know."

"Alright." I made my way up the stairs and through the kitchen. *They're contained...for now. We need to get back into range. We'll need medical assistance and repairs. Half the shit in the storage room is contaminated. We don't know if their blood is harmful. This hallway is a mess. At least they didn't get into control. The girls are okay. Eliza's patching up London.*

"Did it work?" Sophie asked, walking up to me.

"Yes. They're trapped."

"Hyke?"

"Didn't make it. Damien and Kenneth will move his body to the morgue once they're done clearing."

An electrical hum lit the control panel. I walked over to my seat. *Thank fuck, we're back online.* "Power storage is dead. We'll have to wait until solar recharges to get moving."

"How much power will we need?" London asked.

"Twenty percent should be enough to jump the engines. Once they're on, they should help recharge the storage batteries. Hope they weren't too badly damaged."

"If they were?"

"Then we'll have to slowly make our way closer to a sun to charge more efficiently. Forty percent power should be enough to get us back to range and send a distress signal."

"How long will it take before we can get moving?"

"A few hours."

"Too bad we don't have a giant hamster wheel we can run in to generate power."

"Those would take up too much space." I leaned back in my chair and took a deep breath.

"How's your leg feel?" Sophie asked, sitting next to me. "You tore your stitches. I'm going to have to redo them."

"I didn't really feel it."

"Don't do any more running. You need to let this heal."

"No problem. I'm ready for some peace and quiet."

Eliza looked nervous. "We're sure they're contained?"

"Kenneth gave me a long, boring lecture about how impossible it is for the corejackers to get out of that room. We're safe. The boys are going to keep an eye on them for a while."

"Oh," Sophie started. "We never got to try our glowing dye."

I smiled. "We could just tell Damien to dye one of his suits, then throw him in with creatures and see if he lives."

Eliza shook her head. "You yell at Hyke for suggesting violence, then threaten to throw your brother to literal aliens."

"You're right, that isn't really in the spirit of step three."

Chapter 12

9:52 on the clock. Let's see...Owen, deceased. Damien's in control. Sophie and Eliza are in the lab. Kenneth and London are in the cafeteria. All stable. Systems are mostly functional. I slept a lot longer than I should have. Should get some food and check on everything. Just going to throw one of my clean blue jumpsuits on... Time to face whatever chaos this day has decided to bring us.

The hallway was quiet. *At least there's no more blood. Let's see what's for breakfast. Looks like London is standing in the hallway near the break room.*

"Morning, Emma," London said, eating a burrito. "Hungry?"

"Yes."

"Here. Kenneth and I made these."

"You?"

"Relax. Kenneth didn't let me put pepper in anything, unfortunately."

"You are a menace, London." *When was the last time I ate? When was the last time anyone ate a proper meal. I missed actually getting to enjoy food. This is so good.* "How are things going?"

"Calm, surprisingly. Damien has been messing with the power supply and control functions. Kenneth and I have

119

been running between corejackers watch and damage checks on all our lower-level rooms. Eliza has been nervously going over samples, learning what she can about our wild guests, and Sophie has been up since four in the morning, energetically running around the lab, mumbling about plant revitalization."

"Plant revitalization?"

"Nothing downstairs survived. The algae room and the garden are both dead."

"Fuck. At least the oxygen converter should be running again. We should be fine for a while."

London handed me a plate of burritos. "Why don't you go down there and get those two to stop with the science and eat something?"

"Sounds good. Which lab are they in?"

"Two, last I checked. I'll go throw some food at Damien."

Owen would like these. I smiled and walked down the stairs. *I can imagine him as a ghost, bummed out that he can't have any. Damn, I miss him.*

Buckets of soil, clear chemical containers, vials, light fixtures, and muddied pots were strewn about Sophie's desk.

"What have you got there?" I asked, walking up to her.

"Well, I went to check on the plants and algae tanks. Unfortunately, all living material was drained down here, but I found a way to fuse the genetics of the vegetable plants, algae, and my glowing plant, Clarence."

"Fusing genetics. Sounds cool."

She stood up and held out a pot with a strange plant in it. The stems varied in thickness, presenting a dark green color. Its rounded triangular leaves reached upwards, glowing with patches of bright aqua and lime green. "These create four times the oxygen of a normal plant, emit light to deter corejackers, and should still be capable of producing food. I used some of my propagations from the glowing one. The algae components will help them grow quickly."

She's adorable when she gets excited like this.

Eliza turned toward us and smiled. "She's been making a mess all morning."

"Sorry," Sophie said. "I had to create a new soil mixture from some of our void rock samples and electric-safe soil that stays at the perfect level of moistness. It would have been easier if I had more soil options."

Eliza chuckled. "Too bad hardware stores don't deliver out here."

"I should be able to start converting the garden soil so we can grow more plants like this. I might end up running out of rock samples."

"What kind do you need?" I asked.

"Anything similar to the ones we found with Clarence."

"Send the chemical data to the control room and we can get the external computing analyzer started. Maybe we can find some more of your rocks on our way back."

"Perfect!"

I set the tray of burritos down on a clean table. "Now, how about you both take a break and have some breakfast, courtesy of Kenneth and London. Don't worry, London was not allowed to assault the food with pepper this time."

Sophie took off her bird-covered gardening gloves. "Maybe we should hide it from her."

"Then she'd just complain about the food constantly."

"Fair point."

"How have our corejackers been?"

Eliza sat down. "We've been monitoring them for a few days now. Sophie and I have compiled all the notes if you'd like a report. We have some new theories on their biology and intellect."

"Go ahead."

"For starters, their blood is far different from ours. It matches the color of their bodies, possibly so they can hide their injuries. Instead of transferring oxygen, it stores and transfers energy throughout the body. I'd imagine, since they have no mouth, they have no digestive or respiratory systems. They clearly don't need oxygen. I hypothesize their bodies primarily consist of bone and muscle-like structures. No idea yet on how they reproduce. We may be able to know more if we manage to find their origin."

"Okay."

"I believe their claws are mostly made of bone, or at least consist of some sort of hard, durable material. They don't seem able to bend the end of their primary claw, though they can move that secondary appendage, the one similar to a thumb."

"Why would they need those features—eyes, legs, weird hands—if they just need to absorb energy to survive? They look like hunters."

"Maybe their place of origin consists of other living creatures that give off energy. If the planet either doesn't give off any, or gives off very little, they might need to be hunters."

"That would explain why they attacked us. The ship was out of energy; they needed to find more. How do they communicate?"

"I believe they use small bursts of energy, undetectable to us," Eliza continued. "I've documented some odd pulses they emit when near each other. If one emits these pulses, the others will turn toward it and respond with more."

"Okay, so they can chat. Good to know."

"They seem to have surprisingly good sight as well. Not sure if they can see us through the observation window, but they like to look around, evaluate their surroundings. I believe they are fairly intelligent. They're careful. Seem to remember locations. They stare at the radio every now and then, possibly waiting to see if it gives off more energy."

"Did they attack it at all?"

"No. They drained it of power but didn't destroy it. They don't seem constantly violent by any means. I believe they know what's living and what isn't. Electronics can't run so there is no need to attack."

"I'm curious if they know what electronics are, or if they simply know it isn't alive."

"Not sure," she responded. "We will need a better research containment zone to study them further. Can't run advanced tests with the setup we have."

"We prioritized capture. We'll try to get communication with Asrocore, see if they can prepare something for our return."

"They usually have a few pre-made research sites ready."

"Keep me updated, I'm going to check our trajectory." I turned toward Sophie. "Try not to get the lab covered in mud."

She smiled. "No promises."

Never thought I'd still have to deal with mud out in the void. Always grew up thinking ships and stations were spotlessly clean at all times. No one really explained all the biological components needed to maintain healthy environments. That's what I get for going into piloting instead of scientific research.

I walked into the control room to find Damien slowly spinning in his chair, staring at his tablet. "Anything cool?" he asked.

"Eliza thinks they can tell the difference between living organisms and electronics."

"So, they're fairly intelligent?"

"Apparently."

"Do we know if it would be possible to learn some form of communication with them?"

"Not yet. They can communicate with each other, but we don't have the equipment to fully understand it."

"Would be nice if we could convince them to not try and kill us. Give them an inclear device and call it good."

"That would be nice." I sat down. "How much power do we have?"

"Nineteen percent. Not enough for a jump, but we should be able to get moving. How are you feeling?"

"Sore."

"Awake enough to pilot?"

"Don't think I can drive this thing in my sleep?"

He smiled "You probably could. Engines are ready."

"Let's get out of here. Where's the closest star? We'll need something strong enough to charge quickly."

"There's one between us and the D-Six-Zero anomaly. Shouldn't take too long to get to."

"Let's get the distress signal going. Keep an eye on our power levels. Let me know if the power storage kicks back on."

"Got it. It's going to take a few days to get back to range," Damien said.

"Hope we don't run into any more problems."

Chapter 13

"Kenneth..."

"Emma."

"Why?"

He stepped closer and dramatically stared at the long stick wedged diagonally into the frame keeping the door half open.

"Also, how?" I asked.

"Well... I could tell you we were practicing combat again, or..."

Damien peeked his head into view behind Kenneth.

"I could say that we were cleaning and I slipped and accidentally wedged the handle into the frame."

I crossed my arms. "How long have you been stuck in there?"

"Only a minute."

I sighed and stepped closer to the door's control panel, lifting my tablet toward the screen.

Admin access granted to Captain Emma Rown.

The door clicked and slid open as far as it could.

I unwedged the mop handle from the frame and tossed it at Kenneth. "A mere mop handle isn't going to save you from corejackers."

"No, but it's a start."

"You're lucky I can override the door, or I'd have to get London down here to bail you out, and you know how she acted when Damien's door was broken."

"Left me helpless," Damien said, making a sad face. "Abandoned, forlorn, forsaken, jilted."

Kenneth looked toward him. "Well, you should have used a mop handle instead of a plastic alligator."

I crossed my arms and stepped closer. "Maybe I just need to put you both in your place to stop the damage you keep causing."

"How...?"

I grabbed a nearby broom handle and pointed it toward them. "Whose first?"

"You're injured," Kenneth said.

"And I can still kick ass. Get over here and fight me without breaking anything."

He shifted his stance. "Fine."

He has no idea. I still remember all of Owen's moves. I shall not disappoint the spirit of a true exploration warrior.

He lunged forward and swung toward my right side.

I quickly stepped forward and grabbed his weapon, twisting it to offset his balance.

He stumbled to the side and tried to pull it out of my grip.

I grinned. "Feeling outmatched yet?"

"We just started!" He smiled and twisted his body to regain control of his weapon, jumped up and aimed for my shoulder.

I stepped to the side and tapped his foot, unsteadying him again.

His eyes widened with realization. "I didn't know you had such skills."

Damien chuckled. "She was trained by Owen."

Kenneth stepped back and paused. "No, you didn't tell me."

"I thought it would be fun to watch."

"I have no chance."

"Preposterous!" I said, stepping closer. "Don't just give in because I was trained by a legend. Embrace the very essence of that legend. Prove your worth. Show me what Owen would do."

He smiled and stood tall. "For Owen!" He jumped forward and swung again.

Metal-infused wood smacked together with force. Swing after swing was met with equal ferocity.

"Felicitations, Kenneth, but you know not of his tricks." I quickly somersaulted to the side, jumped up, pressed the pole against his shoulders, grabbed his weapon and used it to weaken his legs.

He fell forward. "I respect your skills... Oh, hi London."

I stepped back and straightened my posture. *She looks displeased...*

"You," London started, looking at Kenneth, "are supposed to be fixing the light in here, not breaking more of them."

"I was about to—"

She turned toward me. "And you are not supposed to be jumping around with that leg. You're so lucky you didn't reopen anything."

Damien quietly snuck out the door.

Kenneth smiled. "We will put these down and get right on those lights."

She glared and stepped out.

I took a deep breath and walked toward the flickering panel in front of the middlemost core battery. "So, what were you supposed to be doing?"

"Fixing the light and that panel you're staring at."

"I'll get this if you get that."

"Okay, should just be a loose wire. That's one of the only batteries that survived."

"What percentage?"

"Two of six are working."

"It's at least something."

"That one is fine, just needs the connection wire retaped. I had to do it a couple weeks ago. With all our running around and being battered by anomalies, it must have come loose again."

I pulled off the screen and stared down at the collection of circuitry and tubing. "This small orange one?"

"Yup."

I gently retaped it to the side of the box and reattached the screen. "Looks fine."

"Easiest repair we've ever had to do." He finished tinkering with the light and stepped off his stool. "Done here."

"What's next?"

He pulled a large flexible hose out of the wall. "The dreaded battery cleaning. Takes two people."

I sighed and stepped closer. "I really wish we were allowed robotic assistants for this."

"They still haven't gotten their compassion simulations to work well. You tell them something sad and they just make a crying face for three hours straight while doing work. It's depressing."

"More depressing than having to do manual core battery cleaning?"

"Yes, I've seen it in person. They look like a scolded puppy. People just feel sorry for them and let them do what they want all the time."

"Hopefully the next generation will work better."

"Maybe they already released one, we have been gone for a while. Commander Front did say they were working on an entire new coding system for them."

"Do they have to do that with every gen?"

"Yes, something about code safety regulations and compatibilities with new minerals and such. I never studied intelligent robotics. I'm a ship electrician. London knows more about the coding nonsense."

I kneeled next to one of the dead batteries. "Alright, where's that unreasonably large brush?"

"First off, sit down." He gestured toward my knee. "You have a leg injury. Second, remember to scrub like your life depends on it or Boston will come back just to scold you."

"Giving Owen a chance to steal our coffees."

Kenneth smiled. "He never stole London's."

"Don't tell me: she put pepper in it."

"Yup."

"Space is always strange, but sometimes people are far stranger."

Chapter 14

Damien walked into the control room and sank into his seat. "Morning. How's your leg?

"A little stiff," I responded, tossing one of the plushies at him. "I've had worse."

"How's our power?"

"Still only two batteries. Can't make any fast jumps, but we have enough to use a dash charge. Won't be as good as a full jump, but will still get us back quicker."

"Okay. I'll make sure the maps line up."

"Maybe we should go manual for the image integrated software. I trust your sketches more than this thing's memory drive."

He waved a colored pencil at me. "I got it fixed yesterday. It shouldn't have any issues."

"I'll give the crew a heads-up," I said, grabbing my tablet. "Okay. All have received the message and are getting secure."

"I hope Sophie cleaned up all that soil. Would be a nightmare to deal with in a dash."

"Eliza made her clean it up last night."

"Everything looks good on my end." He walked over to Owen's station. "Fine over here as well. We're clear to dash."

I glanced at the plant in front of him. "Maybe we should get Clarence secured first."

"Good idea." He picked it up and eyed the bottom. "Got any Space Hippo tape?"

"You want rainbows, stars, or cheesecake?"

"Rainbows." He grabbed it from my hand and chuckled. "Maybe we should get some flamingo tape."

"I'm sure we could find some in the craft storage room back at base."

"There, nice and secure."

"Then sit down and remember the rules."

"Don't die."

"Exactly." *Let's see, flip this switch, type in the command, make sure all the sensors are active, and...here we go.*

The overhead lights shifted to a light orange. The ship's dash alarm echoed down the hall, followed by a loudening electrical hum before we jolted forward. *That didn't feel right...*

Emergency alarms blared. The lights went red.

"Ow... What happened? Damien?"

"I don't know. Everything was lined up..."

"Where the hell are we? The pilot protocols are flashing with errors, the locator is glitching, and most of the sensors are going haywire."

"I'm going manual. Give me a sec... Okay, we're not too far from where we were. These constellations match up, though they're far closer now. Looks like it jumped us toward where the *Vision Three* was supposed to be exploring."

"The *Vision* is the older exploration vessel, right?"

"Yeah."

"Hope they aren't dealing with the same problems we are. I told you to run the mapping program manually."

"You were right. I'll start adding in my sketches and help the computer find its way back."

"Thank god for your great memory," I said.

"Thank Mom. She's the one who could recite the entire dictionary."

"And would use that gift to educate us while we were in timeout. Pure torture."

"Yeah, all the words just blurred together after a while. We do have an impressive vocabulary now."

"That we only use for comedic purposes because it was drilled into our brains along with pure boredom."

"Remember what ballyhoo means?"

"Something about an outcry?"

"Usually for a cause or advertising."

"Don't you start tormenting me now."

"Would you rather hear someone spout the dictionary again, or fight a corejacker bare handed?"

"Fight the corejacker... Hold on, what's this?"

"Fuck, there are meteors everywhere," Damien said. "Looks like we almost ran into this mess. Those rocks are just as dark as the D-Six-Zero anomaly."

"Is that a planet?" I asked, gesturing toward a large mass of darkness straight ahead. "Looks like a planetary collision. That mass next to it clearly didn't come off of it. These meteors must be the rest of that chunk. Most likely an old collision. They usually emit vast quantities of energy on impact. These pieces have had time to dissipate."

"There's no sun nearby. I wonder if they were orbiting each other or just happened to collide while flying through space."

"Wait, to the left. That's not a rock."

Shards of broken glass and metal floated around a small triangular ship. Its front end was smashed open. Not a single spark or shred of light.

Just as dark as everything else around here. "The Vision Three..."

"Right at the edge of their map range. I'll start scanning for life."

"Their control window is cracked. Even if they managed to get into suits, they wouldn't have survived for long. Let's get a little closer, see if we can determine what happened."

"We never received a distress call. We're the only other ship out here. Never picked anything up."

"Maybe they weren't able to send one. Anomalies hit fast sometimes."

"The supply ship met with them before us. Think the corejackers started on the *Vision*? They have outer access

135

doors and the ability to land on large meteors. Would make sense if they landed somewhere and left the outer airlock door open too long and something snuck onboard. Do you remember if supply mentioned any issues with the *Vision*?"

"No, but the supply crew were all busy when we docked."

Damien sighed. "Scans are negative. No life. Damn. A whole ship lost to those things. Do we try to recover what we can?"

"We're too badly damaged. Pull up the info logs. Let's see who was on it."

Damien moved over to Owen's station. "Looks like the *Vision* had six crew. Captain Dolores Hyves. Mapping coordinator, Gene Paulus. Defense rep, Gunner Fobbs. Void chem expert, Glina Matt. Mechanic and programmer, Barb Twint. Medical expert and biologist, Gibson Gibsonn. See any bodies?"

"Two. Captain and medic. Do we have any functioning tethers?"

"We should."

"Tether them to their ship so they can be recovered later."

"Maybe we should send a warning down to the lab. Eliza might panic seeing them."

I reached for my tablet. "On it."

"This is a much bigger problem than we can handle. What if supply continued spreading those things? How many ships might be failing right now...?"

"What ship was supply supposed to go to after us?"

"I don't know. They change the order too much. Exploration ships get called back for repairs frequently."

"We should have access to their route plan. Supply is supposed to share it in case a ship needs emergency restocking."

"We're too far from the next zone to get word out to the next ships."

"I'm not thinking of getting word out."

"You want to chase it?" he asked. "We barely survived our trespassers."

"We can at least find out where it's been, where it's going, and stop it from meeting anyone else."

"We might not be fast enough with our damage."

"If we can fix the dash, we might be able to get ahead of it."

He stopped and stared out to the right at another mass of heavily damaged metal in the distance. "We don't have to. That thing looks like it's been through a meteor belt. Rounded shape, green and orange accent paint. The supply ship."

I grabbed the controls, bringing us to a halt. "Damien, see if we can establish communications."

"Sending comm burst. Scanning for life."

"We can't do a wireless evaluation. If there are corejackers on board, it won't respond. We can't connect or we'll lose power again. We'll just have to wait for a response. If we get any, then we can try to get a rescue team in place. We at least know how to deal with these creatures."

"If we don't get a response?"

"Then we unfortunately can't help."

"It looks abandoned. There's damage on the exterior, like something scraped against it."

"Might have hit meteors when they lost power."

He looked back at his screen. "Life scans are all irregular. There are most likely no living humans on that ship."

"How's their core readings?"

"No power, and they have five cores on that thing."

"Damn. They weren't able to recover. There's nothing we can do for it."

"They didn't have a scientific crew on board. Probably had no idea what was going on."

"It's way farther out than it should be," I said, looking down at my screens. "It was supposed to stay along the safety border. How the hell did it get out here? They wouldn't have simply drifted this far without power."

"What if the *Vision* did send out a distress signal? We might have been dark at the time and just didn't see it. Maybe the supply ship came out here to respond."

"Maybe... I don't know, everything seems off. How would the supply ship have lasted longer than us? It presumably had corejacker issues before we did."

"They did have more crew and five core engines. Maybe they were able to last long enough to respond to the *Vision*."

"All just to die alongside them."

"How about we make sure we don't as well?"

"Dad will kill us if we die out here."

"Step three."

"Step three."

Damien closed his eyes and took a deep breath. "I'll look for bodies."

"This ship had thirty crew."

"It's not burst open like the *Vision*. Bodies should all be inside still. Haven't seen any yet."

"If you do, get them tethered, then we'll head for the nearest station. Keep a distress call going. We need to let everyone know to avoid looking for these ships until a proper recall team is trained. Save our location. We will transfer maps to anyone we come across."

"I'll tether a warning beacon to it, so if any other ships end up out here, they'll know to leave it alone."

"Label it a biohazard. Defense ships are more likely to leave that than an invaded ship."

"True. I wonder how Asrocore is going to react to our corejackers."

"They'll probably set up a research division, build a containment site, have an exploration team search for their home planet, or wherever they came from."

"How did multiple creatures sneak onto the *Vision* without being detected? It isn't that big."

"Our technology doesn't pick up on them. My guess is the crew were a little too reliant on it. Maybe they didn't do enough visual checks on the ship. Some crews get lazy and assume the sensors and monitors are accurate."

He reached for a panel. "Well, looks like I'm going to have to rewire a few things before we jump again. We might be here for a bit. Good opportunity to observe the planetary collision, get a few samples, and see what we're dealing with."

I stood and headed for the door. "I'll check on everyone." *I wonder if the girls can see it from the lab windows. Eliza's probably scared. At least they'll have a better idea what those scratch marks could be.*

London met me in the hallway. "Saw the warning. What's going on?"

"We found the *Vision Three* and the supply ship. Both are lost. Bodies have been tethered. Damien is fixing our dash systems so we can get back to base."

"Both ships?"

"Thirty-six dead, not including our own. We're pretty sure the creatures started on the *Vision*, spread to the supply, then us."

"What is the supply ship doing way out here?"

"Current theory is that they responded to a distress call from the *Vision*."

"That makes sense."

"Do you know what ship supply was headed to next?"

"The *Gladiator Orion*, I think, but they were farther out. I doubt they had time to get to the *Orion* and get all the way out here in that length of time."

"Then there should hopefully not be any more ships with these creatures on board."

"That's a relief."

"I'm heading down to check in with the girls."

"Okay, I'll relay the info to Kenneth."

Thirty-six more. Guess that makes it...fifty-nine? Yeah, fifty-nine. I wonder if anyone else counts how many dead they've encountered. Most people count missions, stations, ships, near-death experiences. Maybe the coroners count. They'd have to for reports.

"What happened?" Sophie asked, watching me walk in.

"Dash launch failed. Mapping system glitched out and almost ran us into a mess of a broken planet."

"Do we know where we are?"

"Yes, we're not too far from familiar stars but we have one more issue. We found the *Vision Three* and the supply ship floating damaged among the rocks. No signs of life."

Eliza's eyes widened. "They're... Are you sure?"

"As sure as we can be. There is no active power, no communications, and no way for us to dock to evaluate. We're too badly damaged ourselves."

"What do we do?"

"Damien is manually rewriting the maps. We need you two to evaluate the structures in this area. Seems there are unusual signatures messing with our systems again."

"We never get a break out here..."

"It wasn't all bad until we found the D-Six-Zero."

"And now everything is chaos."

"Welcome to the void. I was hoping you two could evaluate the scratch marks on the side of the *Astral Supply Four*. They looked weird to me. Not like typical meteor marks."

Eliza pulled up our exterior camera feed on her computer. "No, they aren't."

Sophie stepped closer. "Almost looks more like claw marks. Large ones. Maybe something hit it...or moved it."

"I don't like the sound of that."

"If something did, it would have had to be pretty big. The supply ship is bigger than most exploration vessels."

"That's not terrifying to think about."

"We don't know if there are other creatures."

"Do you know how big the corejackers are supposed to be?"

Sophie pulled up scan images of the corejackers on her tablet. "Kenneth had to remove the large-scale scanner from the observation room, so I only have basic scans and blood samples. Based on their internal bone-like structures and blood chemistry, I'm fairly certain our corejackers are full size."

"There might be something much larger out there." Eliza's eyes widened. She quickly turned back toward her monitor. "I'll start collecting and evaluating rock samples."

"Go easy on the mercury, at least."

I turned toward Sophie. "How are your little plant experiments doing?"

She grabbed a small pot with a blue plant inside. "Great. Oxygen levels are increasing in this room. I can start placing these around the ship, if you'd like to help."

"Of course." I picked up a tray of pots. "Lead the way."

She stepped out and turned left. "We don't have enough for every room yet. I'd like them all to be at least this big first. I already placed some in the oxygen room, so we can head to the engine room, then upstairs."

"They're growing fast. Any concerns about them growing too big?"

"Most of the plant is edible, so we can trim them down for food as needed."

"You are too smart, Sophie." *Glad to hear that familiar hum, the dripping of fluid into the cooling cells. All of the lights are on. The monitor panels are working. The only thing missing is the sound of a grumpy old man mumbling and smacking things with an antique wrench that surprisingly works on most of the components. He'd probably prefer talking to these plants than other people.*

"Here should be fine," Sophie said, stopping next to the main stairs. "Not too close to the core engines, and still accessible for watering."

"How often do we need to water them?"

"Once every two weeks should be fine."

"They need anything aside from water?"

"No. They can even survive a few months without light."

"How does that work?"

"Most of Clarence's cells are capable of recycling their own light in order to self-power their structures."

"That's pretty useful," I said, following her up the stairs.

"What are you two up to?" London asked, standing at the top.

"Sophie made some badass plants that will help with oxygen and food, and are also corejacker proof. We're placing them around the ship."

"Wow. Need help?"

Sophie handed her two pots. "Can you place these in the kitchen and break room? Emma and I will set the last two in the personnel corridor and control room."

"Sure. You know Kenneth is going to want to name them all. He still has that label maker he used to name all the old plants."

"Good," I said. "It will help keep him busy."

Sophie walked down the hallway and placed a plant next to her bedroom door. This one had dark green stems holding up skinny, speckled oval leaves. "The control room one can go wherever you'd like."

"It can go to the right at the edge of the viewing window. Is this thing going to grow onto any nearby surfaces?"

"It shouldn't, though I can't completely rule it out. We are dealing with void plant genetics."

"If it starts to, I'll threaten to cook it with dinner."

She chuckled. "I'm sure that will work."

"You never know, maybe that void plant can hear us."

"It doesn't have those kinds of structures, though I wouldn't be surprised if we end up finding a plant that can hear."

"What if they talk as well? As cool as that initially sounded, I don't know if I'd want a plant that mimics us. Especially if it tried mimicking Kenneth's singing."

"You know he would want to duet with it."

"He would," I said, walking into the control room.

"What's that?" Damien asked, looking at the lime green and aqua plant in my arms.

"Our new oxygen friend," I said, setting it down. "We have a few strewn about the ship."

"Has Kenneth named them yet?"

"Not yet."

"You two going to stay and chat?"

"No."

"Come on, I'm losing my sanity."

"Finish the mapping and we can chat all you want."

"Why don't I teach you how to do this so you can help me next time?"

"I'm not as good with programming. Besides, we should probably head back down and check on Eliza. She can only stress-stare at rocks for so long."

"Good luck, Damien," Sophie said, leading the way out. "Maybe a talking plant would be good for Damien."

"Or Owen. Could you imagine a plant constantly telling all of his stories..." *Owen...*

Sophie placed a hand on my shoulder, noticing my shift in mood. "I'm sure he would try to teach it all sorts of things."

"Yeah."

She turned toward the kitchen door. "I can hear Kenneth excitedly going through names for the plants. I'm sure they'll all be labeled by tomorrow."

"Let's not tell him where they all are. Make it a scavenger hunt for him."

"Sounds fun," she said, following me into the break room.

"Hopefully Damien won't challenge him to another mop handle duel over the right to name them..." I stepped down the stairs and into the lab.

Eliza was sitting at her desk, staring at a rock. "Hmm..."

"Hmm?" I asked.

"Hmmmmmmmm."

"Hmmmmmmmm?"

"Odd," she said, turning toward us.

"What is it?" I asked.

She handed me one of the samples. "Notice anything unusual?"

The rock gently clung to my hand. "Yeah."

"I believe it was part of the planet's core. Seems to have similar qualities to Kethon, pulling things toward it, but not quite as strong."

"Are they all like that?"

"Most of them, though I have found something far more interesting on one of the larger samples." She walked over to the scanning chamber, gesturing toward a larger rock. "The scanners picked up biological material on its surface. Heavily decomposed, though it matches the genetic structure of the corejackers. There are even traces of plant matter as well. My guess is that they were originally from one of those planets. There may have been an entire ecosystem."

Sophie stared at the analyzer screen. "The plant matter is too heavily decomposed for computer reconstruction. Their cell patterns are interesting, almost like it was a non-light-based plant."

"No light?"

"Yeah. They pull energy up from their roots instead of getting it from light. It's not the first time we've seen plants like this, though these structures are...familiar."

I looked at the screen showing a close-up image of the rock's surface. Next to it was a smaller screen covered in scientific words that were entirely too long.

"Wait..." Sophie ran to her desk, grabbed her tablet, then returned. "I know these structures. They're the same."

Eliza stepped closer and peered down at the tablet. "What is this older scan from?"

"Clarence. The sample I got it from must have been a part of the broken planet. Smaller pieces are often shot out into the void on collision."

"I know some space plants can survive planetary collisions, but how would the corejackers have survived? You'd think they would have been overwhelmed by the amount of energy coming out of colliding planets." Eliza began pacing. "What if they were able to travel through space before their planet collided? Their survivors could have been off-planet when it happened."

"We've only seen them on objects so far."

"Maybe they can float between objects. If they aren't too far apart, and they leap just right, they might just go from rock to rock."

"How'd they get off-planet in the first place?"

"I'll let you two debate science," I said. "I don't want to be away from control for too long with all the problems we're having."

Sophie looked at me. "We'll keep you updated."

Wonder how much longer until Damien is done. My leg is getting sore from going up and down the stairs over and over again. Too bad we don't have an elevator on this thing.

I walked into the control room. "Finish mapping yet?"

Damien sat in his chair, staring at the broken planet out the window with a bored expression. "Almost. Have to wait for the software to finish analyzing. Might take a while. Been staring at the mess of void stones for a few minutes."

"Anything interesting happen?" I asked.

"No," he responded. "Just a bunch of floating rocks."

"Eliza said there are traces of biomaterial on the rock samples that matches our corejackers."

"Might be their origin?"

"Possibly. Let's get a closer look." I sat down, carefully maneuvering our ship into the meteor ring.

"Is that a good idea?"

"I'm not going too far, just past these first few rocks. Sheild buffers are active, and we don't have void access, so we should be fine."

"If we die, I'm going to leave a ghost note for Dad, explaining that it was your fault."

"See anything yet?"

"Not... Wait, I'm getting something on the scanner. Movement to the right, about ten yards ahead. It's not a meteor."

Our lights illuminated the dark rocks, exposing oily colored masses darting around the surfaces, trying desperately to avoid the light.

"Looks like we found where they're from," he continued.

"Let's..."

The ship shook. The control panel flashed with emergency lights.

"Shit, something hit us. Damien, hit the flood lights."

"Not responding. They must have been damaged."

"We can't dash without the mapping software."

"I can tell it to go off the sketches alone. It won't be precise, but it might work."

"Do it."

Fuck, now I have to try and steer us out of a crowded meteor plane while avoiding aliens. Great. I promise, Dad, we're trying. "Can we see what hit us yet? Couldn't have been corejackers."

"I can't tell; they're messing with the scanner." He turned toward the main camera screen. "Fuck... Nope, that's not a corejacker."

Shit.

Its body was long and slender. Blue strands waved above its pointed head. Three thick tail-like structures trailed behind it. It had two large arms with thin claw-like appendages similar to the corejackers.

"That's a lot bigger," Damien said. "I don't see eyes..."

"Must have been what hit us."

The ship shook again. Another creature rammed us from above. The screen flashed *Shield error.*

Damien scrambled to keep his tablet from falling. "They're weakening the shield every time they hit it. Must be able to absorb far more energy than the corejackers."

"How many are there?"

"Two so far."

"Can we outrun them?"

"Possibly, if we do a longer dash. It would require a set location for the autopilot."

"The anomaly. It's not too far away. It's in your sketches and the computer already uses it as a landmark."

"Setting to dash to the D-Six-Zero anomaly."

The ship jerked forward. Everything went dark.

Chapter 15

Trees swayed overhead. Thunder jolted through the air, connecting the clouds with strings of light. The flash illuminated the blood on my leg, sending a wave of panic through me.

The tree... The lake... "Mom?"

"Emma? Emma!"

"Damien..." *Damien? Damien, Owen, Sophie, Eliza, London, Kenneth, Boston... No, Boston was...*

I slowly opened my eyes, watching small sparks fly out of one of the panels. *Why am I on the floor?*

"You okay, Emma?" Damien asked, helping me sit up. "One of them hit us as we started the dash. You got knocked out of your seat."

"I think I'm fine."

"Navigational failure, broken planet, more aliens. I don't think that could have gone more egregiously."

"Means catastrophic failure, right?"

"Right. You still have your head."

"I'm sure I'd still remember Mom's dictionary torment no matter how damaged my memory gets." I leaned on the control panel. "We're required to wear seatbelts back home, but don't have any out here where they could be extremely useful."

"Our ships don't get into as many accidents as cars do. Void pilots are far better trained than civilians."

"Yeah, that's true."

"We made it to the anomaly. New stabilization tech is doing its job, so far haven't seen our new friends. London and Kenneth are fixing a flaw in the second core. We'll have to wait here for a while before we can move again."

"Set our engines to low power."

"I have the girls evaluating the images we got of our new friends. I was thinking of calling them phantomjacks. They don't show up on the scans, and they float menacingly through space."

"Okay."

He handed me a cup of water. "Now we wait and hope we weren't followed."

"Feels like we're playing a weird game of hide and seek."

"You sure you're okay? I can get Sophie to take a look at you."

"I'm fine. Was only out for a moment...right?"

"Couple minutes. You have that look. Did you see it again?"

"Just for a moment. I'm getting better at not chasing the memory. I thought it would go away being out here. No windstorms or rain to remind me. No trees. Just the sight of blood and recurring nightmares."

"You been able to sleep well lately?"

"Better since we contained the corejackers. Having Sophie next to me helps."

"Does she know?"

"No, it hasn't come up yet. I try not to wake her if a nightmare wakes me up."

"She'll figure it out eventually, especially if you end up dating."

"I'll tell her about it later."

"Owen would probably lecture you about taking chances and jumping after every opportunity when you can."

"Well, he's not here to boost morale anymore or tell stories about his life."

"I guess we should start telling tales of his adventures. The great Owen Kellner. Man of the void. He who tackled the stars."

"He'd like that."

"Wait," Damien said, staring at the camera screen. "I've got visual. Two phantomjacks are approaching."

"How the hell did they follow us this far?"

"They might be able to detect our power source. I remember Boston mentioning something about the kind of power we use leaving a trail."

"If they get too close, we'll start priming another dash."

"Where to?"

"Back to the main map range. We'll send out a distress signal."

"Starting to wish we had weapons on this thing. The only thing Hyke and I ever agreed on."

"We're supposed to be a peaceful research vessel. Our main conflict protocol is to run and signal for help."

"Hold on...they're slowing down... They stopped."

"Why aren't they getting closer?" I asked.

"I don't know, but it's creepy."

You going to move? Just want to stare at us? They attacked before, maybe they want to analyze the area first. Are you smart enough to check for traps?

We sat in the unsettling silence for a few minutes, each of us staring at a creature. They had stopped on either side, holding distance.

Damien broke the silence. "Guess I can check 'having an alien staring contest' off my bucket list."

"Sounds like a fun list."

"Their claws look similar to the marks on the side of the supply ship. You think they moved it?"

"Possibly. Maybe they wanted to lure us in. The corejackers seem fairly smart. These guys could be just as intelligent."

Eliza ran in. "Stay close to the anomaly! The blood sample we got from the injured corejacker reacted to the D-Six-Zero samples, causing an electrical surge. If these creatures have similar blood chemistry, the anomaly will electrocute them if they get too close."

"Wouldn't they just absorb it?" I asked.

"They can't. Whatever energy the D-Six-Zero is emitting causes disruptions to their systems. The three we have downstairs are all lying down. Our ship gives them enough protection not to be badly shocked, but it's still hurting them."

"We passed by this thing before. I wonder if it affected them then as well."

"Maybe that's why they attacked us when they did. Our proximity to the anomaly might have harmed them enough to make them desperate for energy."

"That's good to know, but how long are we going to be stuck here?"

"They have to leave eventually."

"So do we."

"Maybe we can scare them off."

"How?" I asked.

"How many scanner bots do we have?"

"Three."

"Load them up with rocks from the D-Six-Zero, then have them chase our friends around. See if that's enough to scare them off."

"Fuck, okay." Damien grabbed a controller. "Video games really do pay off out here."

"They're watching the bots," I said. "Wonder if they know what we're doing." *Or if they even know the bots are controlled by us. No idea what they can understand. The bots might just seem like smaller creatures to them? Either way, they're watching. They look almost...hesitant. Sparks have started coming off the bots. The creatures are backing away.*

"That was easier than I expected," Damien said, smiling.

"Bring the bots back to the ship. We'll load up on space rocks to help deter any other visitors we might encounter. Then let's head back to Core Nine, report our findings, and repair the floodlights."

"What if we use all three bots to get one large sample? These rocks aren't dangerous, are they?"

"No," Eliza responded. "They don't emit anything harmful to humans."

"Good."

"I'll go back down to monitor our corejackers while you're doing this. I'll have to make sure the rock you get doesn't kill them."

"Any way we can protect them?"

"We still have those rubber fitness pads right?"

"Should still be in the gym."

"I can put those up to shield them."

"Alright," Damien started. "Let's get ourselves a rock."

One rock didn't sound that bad. Just one harmless space rock. But of course, Damien had to be extra.

"Uh…" I stared out the window. "I don't think it's going to fit in the sample airlock. Might have to get something smaller."

"Just use the main airlock," Damien suggested.

"We can't open that thing unless it's connected to an airlock terminal."

"I can override the commands."

"You sure it's safe?"

"It'll be fine. I'll ask London and Kenneth to man the door. We need a good-sized rock in case we run into anything bigger."

"Fair point." *We're already fucked, so why not.* "Be careful."

He smiled. "Always am." He grabbed his tablet. "Okay, letting them in on the plan... London's calling me a hazard... Kenneth thinks it's a good idea. Telling them to wave at the camera when they're ready."

I didn't expect to be watching camera footage of London sabotaging the door controls so we could get a large rock that we are mostly certain is safe to be around.

"Okay, bringing the rock in..." he continued. "London's closing the outer door...and we're good."

"Systems are fine, no errors or emergency signals."

"Were you expecting catastrophe?"

"On an already badly damaged ship with alien invaders and a sleep-deprived crew?"

"Fair point. At least we're safer now. Is that thing going to mess with our dreams?"

"Probably."

"More flamingoes."

"Yup. We secure?" I asked, watching London give a thumbs up to the camera.

"Yeah, mostly," she responded with her tablet. "It's a little too big to move now that it's inside with the gravity system on. We're kind of stuck until we dock."

"Asrocore isn't going to like that."

"At least we're bringing back enough to keep the ship safe. We might want to be careful doing more dashes. Keep the inner door closed, just in case."

Chapter 16

London smiled. "Fuck yes, pancakes. Kenneth, you're the best."

He sat at the table and nodded.

"Morning," I said, walking into the cafeteria. "How are you feeling?"

"Not too bad," London responded. "Those things don't hurt as much as they make you tired."

"Yeah, my leg has been harder to move ever since, especially with the stairs."

"We should have an elevator."

"Then we'd all be lazy."

"Have any weird dreams?"

"Glitchy but no pink birds. You?"

"Same. The rocks clearly aren't as powerful as the whole anomaly. You going to eat?"

"I should check on power."

She handed me a plate. "Eat first."

"I can—"

"No, sit and eat. Right here. No screens or weird rocks."

"Okay. It has been a while since I've had pancakes."

She sat across from me. "No one's better at making them than Kenneth."

I looked out the window, studying the shapes of dim, flickering lights. *We should be back in the main map range soon. We've been so busy the last few days. Damien and I haven't gotten around to naming the constellations on this side. One of them looks like an umbrella.*

Kenneth started leaning forward. His chin rested on his hand. A soft snore escaped his nose.

London smiled and grabbed a large pancake, slowly placing it over his head. "Let's see how long that stays on," she whispered.

"Does Kenneth usually move much in his sleep?"

"No..." She giggled and grabbed a couple more large pancakes. "That's better. He is now the king of pancakes."

"Well, if he is the king, we should make him a proper crown." I grabbed the top two pieces and cut out the centers, then used them to make smaller triangles.

London rummaged through one of the drawers before returning with a small cardboard box. "Here, use these to keep them in place."

"Toothpicks, brilliant. Here we go... One on the front, one on the back, and now a couple on each side. Perfect!" *Just another day out in the void.* "He should probably go back to bed."

"And miss this excitement?" London joked. "Where's the syrup?"

"Kenneth's hogging it," I said, carefully grabbing it from in front of his face. "Did he name all the plants yet?"

"Yup, there's Clarence the Second and Tulip."

161

"Tulip?"

"He giggled at that name for a solid five minutes. He hasn't been sleeping enough. The one in the engine room is Boston, the one in the kitchen is Hyke, and the one in the break room is Owen. He sat there for a while and talked to that one while putting on the label."

Boston. Owen. Hyke.

The ship jerked to a sudden stop.

"Fuck, what now?" I rushed out of the room and down the hall.

Damien was standing in the control room with a guilty smile. "Sorry. I tried to repair one of the sensors and the ship glitched a bit. We're okay now. It was just a momentary thing."

"I honestly can't remember what it's like being on a functional ship anymore."

"Think Asrocore will be able to get this thing repaired properly after all the patchwork we've done to it?"

"I'm sure they will, but you know they'll be complaining about it."

"Most exploration vessels return with some problems. They should be used to it by now."

"You'd think."

A small light began flashing on the main board. "We're getting a comm signal," Damien said.

"From which ship?"

"The *E.E.E.* Still don't know what *E.E.E* stands for."

"Why don't you ask the crew?"

"I did. They didn't know, either."

I grabbed the comm and stared out at the large, round ship equipped with a variety of weapons, robotic arms, and towing equipment. "This is Captain Emma Rown aboard the *R.E.L.I-X*. We have an emergency situation on board. Multiple casualties. Do you read?"

"Clear, *R.E.L.I-X*. This is Gloria Stenlot, captain of the *E.E.E*. What's your situation?"

"We have dangerous alien life forms on board. Currently contained in one of our observation rooms. We believe they came from the *A.S.F*. We need assistance getting back to base."

"Do you need us to send a support team to you?"

"No. Keep yourselves at a distance, just in case. The creatures can absorb energy. Are there any other ships in the area?"

"None."

"Do you have any prototype inclear lights on board?"

"Yes."

"These things are smart. If we go dark, you can send an emergency crew out heavily armed. The life forms can take a fair amount of damage without going down. They hate light, so make sure to have the inclear lights on hand. They can't drain those."

"Roger. Setting a course for Core Nine. We'll keep our emergency team on standby."

"Glad we ran into you, Gloria. Were you out on a patrol?"

"We were sent out to search for the *Astral Supply Four* after it missed its scheduled meeting with another research vessel. The supply ship's captain had reported odd power malfunctions on the ship, then went silent."

"We met with it on schedule. Didn't realize creatures had boarded our ship until a few days later. We saw the *A.S.F* and *Vision Three* on our way back. No survivors, heavily damaged. We believe the creatures were on the *Vision* first, spread to the *A.S.F*, and then to us. We should send out emergency signals to all other ships that are on the supply ship's roster."

"Will do. You two doing okay? How's Owen? Usually he's chatting his mustache off."

Owen... I looked down at my tablet, staring at the single word next to his name. *Deceased.* "He didn't make it. We lost our engineer and defense expert as well."

"Damn... I'm sorry. Owen was one of the best. I know you two were close to him."

"Thanks, Gloria."

"Is the rest of your crew alright?"

"Two wounded. Four physically unharmed. No one is well rested."

"Sleep ghosts most people when they leave the comforts of a planet or station. All except for the crazy ones."

Damien smiled. "I'm sure Owen didn't lose even a wink of sleep. Man wasn't scared of anything. Should have asked his secret to zero anxiety before he died."

"Get one of those Ouija boards and ask him," Gloria suggested.

"Good idea. Could you imagine if we had space ghost hunters? How many permits would they need to have to investigate ships?"

"Just four, actually," I answered.

"How the hell do you know that, Emma?" Gloria asked.

"Me and some friends did research on it back on the old S.E.T Zero-One-Nine. Had enough weird paranormal encounters to look into it. A couple of my friends actually considered starting a paranormal group. Seems that Asrocore didn't really think about the paranormal when making all of their regulations."

"How much time do you two spend actually working?"

"We just caught intelligent alien life," Damien said. "I think we've done enough work."

"Says the one sword fighting Kenneth with mop handles on his days off," I added. "You've been an absolute menace to the lights."

"Who usually wins?" Gloria asked.

"Me," Damien answered with a smile. "I've had more training."

"Kenneth's still young. He might surpass you one day."

"Not if I don't teach him all my tricks."

"If you don't, Casey will."

"Casey could kick all our asses."

"Hold on a second, you two," Gloria said, causing a few seconds of silence. "Alright, my crews are set. Are you ready to head out? How well can you move? Are you able to perform a jump?"

"No, our power storage is damaged," I responded.

"Is your ship's integrity high enough to do a grid jump? We have the power cables and spare energy cycles."

"Do you have outer access on that thing?"

"Of course. We do randomly selected void training all the time. Helps keep the crew on their toes."

"Glad I'm not on your crew," Damien said.

"We won't have to dock. Just stop as close to us as you can and I'll have a team start preparing."

Damien turned toward me. "We sure that's safe? I know we have the creatures disconnected from our power grid, but they like to surprise us and we don't want to risk Gloria's ship going powerless too."

"We have four different types of energy converters," Gloria reassured. "And we're close to two different suns. Our solar reserves alone can jump us if needed."

"Alright."

I turned off our comm and glanced at Damien. "Glad the steering on this thing still works perfectly. Gloria would definitely fight me with a broom if I damaged her ship."

"And she'd win," he added.

"Should be close enough," Gloria said. "I've got four people ready to head out and connect. Try not to surprise them too much."

"What?" Damien asked. "Are you sending us recruits? Not all of your crew can handle a little surprise?"

"Keep sassing me, Damien, and I'll throw a suit on you and dump you into the void before we jump."

"That sounds lonely..."

"Maybe it wouldn't be so bad," I said. "You might get killed by creatures before you starve to death. Those big ones don't seem to mind traveling long distances for energy."

"I'd be a mere snack to those things."

"What things?" Gloria asked.

"I'll send you the footage. So far we've seen two types of energy-absorbing creatures, the ones on our ship and big ass fuckers we found at an old planetary collisions site."

"Alright... Got the footage... Shit. Those things look wild. About the size of a bus."

"Wasn't the most relaxing thing to see barreling toward us."

"I could take them. This ship's prepped for anything, just put on the shield buffer and we're on."

"They break through shield buffers. Those things can tank your energy faster than you can say hello. I hope we don't run into any more of them. How close are we to getting out of here?"

"We're connected. All four jump cables are secured. Computers are talking. Everything looks good, just waiting for my guys to get back into the ship and we can go."

"Good. I'm ready to be done with peril, at least for a little while."

"Your crew ready to jump? Might want to have everyone secured, in case you experience issues."

I grabbed my tablet. "Sending notifications now."

"That fancy new ship of yours ever do a grid jump before?"

"One. Owen tested it before we left. Worked fine."

"Good."

"Everyone's responded to the jump order. We're secure. Good to go, Gloria."

"Alright."

"Connection is strong. Our power is maximizing. Cables look good. Here we go."

"Try not to black out this time," Damien said.

"What's he talking about?" Gloria asked.

"We had turbulence during a dash, and I got knocked out of my seat," I answered. "I'll be fine as long as we don't get smacked around again."

"Okay. If you start feeling off, let Damien take over."

"You know how bad his piloting is."

"Yes, but a bad pilot is still better than an unconscious one."

"Debatable."

"Okay, we're moving. Jumping in five, four, three, two, one."

I watched bright colors cover the window. *Ow. Still gives me a headache. Maybe jumping not long after getting knocked out wasn't the best idea. I'm still conscious, at least. Connection's still good and the cables are holding. Just got to make sure we don't get too far apart. Power is destabilizing... Doesn't look too bad. I'll keep an eye on it. Just a couple hours and we should be back in range of the station. There shouldn't have been more infected ships, but we can't be certain until they all check in at base. We're riding on theories right now. Fuck... Didn't think we'd be going back to the station with three bodies. I know casualties are normal, but I doubt anyone expected Owen to be one of them. He knew most of the people at our station. Helped train half of its crew.*

"You still good over there, Rown siblings?" Gloria asked.

"Still conscious," Damien said. "For now. Emma looks a bit rough. I might overthrow her."

I glared at him. "Give me a mop handle and I'll smack those mutinous thoughts out of you while still piloting this thing smoother than you could dream."

"In a fighting mood, Emma?"

"You know she'd win," Gloria added.

"I still have full function of all my limbs."

"She break that leg again?"

"I didn't break it this time," I said.

"Damn, girl, you trying to be like Casey? I don't know how much more damage that leg can take before you'll have to replace it."

"Then Casey can join me in kicking both your asses with our prosthetics."

Damien smiled. "I missed this."

Gloria laughed. "Well, you've got another couple hours of banter before we're done. I'll fill you in on our latest gossip."

"Oh, I'm ready."

Chapter 17

"He didn't..."

"He did," Gloria said, laughing. "Four times."

"Four!" Damein responded. "Are you sure?"

"He tried a fifth time, but it didn't work."

"Five perfect shots in void basketball. I don't believe you."

"We got it on camera. One of our bragging points to flaunt when we get back."

"We're almost there," I said. "How about you two stop gossiping and prepare docking procedures?"

"Already on it," Glora responded. "Welcome home, *R.E.L.I-X* crew."

Damien looked out at the dark grey mass in front of us, highlighted in florescent green trim. "There's the station. Looks good. Can't wait to get inside and relax. Hope no one exploded my bed while I was gone."

"Did you piss off Casey before you left?"

"Not that I know of, but my luck hasn't been all that great recently. We should be good to disconnect, Gloria."

"Roger, Rown siblings. Unhooking the cables now. You're free. Good luck dealing with the commanders."

"We'll need it..." I looked at Damien. "Go make sure everyone's ready."

"Got it."

I grabbed the comm. "Core Nine. Do you read?"

"Clear, *R.E.L.I-X*," a husky voice responded. "We received your distress signal. We have a team in place to handle your visitors."

"We will need help clearing the airlock bay first..."

"Why?"

"We might have shoved a large boulder into it to deter giant hostile aliens..."

They sighed. "Alright. Head to the E-Two dock. We will require your ship to be fully scanned before opening."

"Glad to hear from you, Marty."

"You as well, Emma."

Damien walked back in. "Everyone's already suited up." He sat down and put his feet up. "Can't wait to sneak into our candy stash. Hope Casey didn't eat it all while we were gone."

"Do a quick sensor check. I want to make sure we're actually functioning well enough to dock safely."

"I could always dock us if you're not feeling confident."

I glared at him. "We're already damaged enough."

"I could at least use the practice. I didn't crash the last couple times..."

"Sensors?"

"Fully functional. We're clear."

"Good." *Approaching the dock... Lining up with the ramp... Adjusting power...and we're on.* "I'm surprised that didn't end in catastrophe, to be honest."

Damien stood and fixed his black jumpsuit. "Ready?"

"Ready."

"Everyone should already be waiting at the dock."

One last check... Damien and I are walking out of control. London, Kenneth, Sophie, and Eliza are all by the exit. Owen, Hyke, and Boston are gone... Three deaths. Three bloodied bodies in the morgue. Three too many.

Sophie grabbed my hand as I walked in. "You okay?"

"It's never easy reporting losses."

"I understand."

Damein tapped my shoulder. "The rock is out of the way. Time to go. Everyone, line up."

Two months, eight days since we've stepped off the ship, seen other people, slept in a far safer bed. Feels just as good as heading out sometimes. We get to tell stories and chow down on good food.

"I wonder if Casey is still here," London said, walking off the ship. "I've missed kicking their ass at video games."

"You never win," Kenneth said, glaring at her.

"I will this time."

"Sure."

There's Commander Front on the platform, wearing his dark purple jumpsuit. Looks like they finally made up their minds on the new commander symbol. The typical Asrocore sun symbol in front of X shape circuitry with more tailless arrow circuitry pointing toward it. He's also wearing his signature "I'm tired but still in charge" expression.

"Emergency crews will begin decontaminating and repairing your ship," he said. "Brief me on your incident, Captain Rown."

"We discovered alien life had boarded our ship after a catastrophic power failure. Unfortunately, three died during the mission. Robert Boston, Owen Kellner, and Mitch Hyke. The three creatures are on board, trapped in the lab one observation room. We also witnessed another type of life form out in the void, footage of which is recorded on the ship. We believe we have found their place of origin: an old planetary collision sight. They seem to habit the meteor debris that floats around the destroyed planets."

"We will have all footage analyzed. Anything further?"

"Yes. We located the *Vision Three* and the *Astral Supply Four* in the planetary debris. The *Vision's* control room was heavily damaged. No survivors. The *A.S.F* seemed to receive mostly internal damage. Scans were all negative, likely also no survivors. We were too badly damaged to recover anything from either ship. Bodies were tethered."

"Known causes for these losses?"

"We believe the creatures started on the *Vision,* spread to *A.S.F,* then our ship. It's possible the supply ship went off course to respond to a distress from the *Vision.* Our ship was offline for several days, so we do not have proof one was sent out, but it could explain the supply vessel being so far out. We also noted scratch marks on the side of the *A.S.F,* likely from the larger creatures we

174

encountered. It's possible they pulled the ship into the debris of the broken planet either to lure or bring energy to others."

"Retrieval options?"

"Retrieval might be possible with proper planning and equipment."

"Is your ship's mapping software functional?"

"Yes. Some areas had to be repaired manually, but map transfer should have no problems."

"Any further information that needs to be discussed at this time?"

"No, sir."

"Very well. Make sure all of you are seen by medical and get some rest. I will call a meeting once I have evaluated your reports and the status of your ship. Eliza and Sophie, you will go to Eli to make sure he knows everything he needs to know about your captives. You are dismissed."

I sighed. "Time to relax."

Damien put a hand on my shoulder. "After we get through the scan doors."

"Shouldn't take too long. They upgrade them constantly, so we aren't stuck in a decontamination room for thirty minutes every time we want to get to our dock."

He followed me through the door. "Ooh, looks like they put new lights up."

"Probably full spectrum for the eval cams."

"Must be a boring job sitting at a desk watching decom rooms all day."

"I heard a rumor that the research department makes people do that job when they mess up. Punishment for making big messes or being an ass."

"Really?" He glared at the camera. "What did you do, huh?"

"We'll never know."

"You have an in on the research department. I'm sure they'd tell Sophie."

"Probably."

He glanced at the camera once more before following me out. "At least they get to see our beautiful faces. Hang in there."

"You can always go keep them company. Tell them about our latest adventure."

"I've got gossip to engage in. Looks like a couple other research vessels are in. We should see who's hanging around the E-section break room."

I turned the corner and stopped. "Looks like we've been found."

A pair of black and white cats sat on the floor. One was chubby with a large patch of black that went diagonal across his face, wrapped around his back, and trailed down one front leg and covered most of his tail. The other was scrawny, mostly white with black patches over one eye, ear, and the end of his tail. Both were wearing purple shirts with gold trim and the commander symbols on the back.

Damien reached out and picked up the chubbier one. "My favorite boys. How are you, Moo? Making sure everyone is working efficiently?"

"That's more Milkshake's job," I said, petting Moo's scrawny, wide-eyed brother.

"Yeah, Moo is more the adventurous type. Milkshake just looks like he's watching every particle in the air at all times."

"Wonder if he was born with that wild look in his eyes."

"We'll never know. Their origin is a mystery."

I pushed open the break room door. *There it is, the sound of laughter, footsteps, properly functioning air vents. The smell of sanitation spray, freshly cleaned jumpsuits, and whatever snacks people have been sneaking around. No more silence and blood.*

Damien turned toward the window. "Looks like the *Wandering Eagle* just got back. Looks badly damaged. Dusty should be around here somewhere... Ah, there!" He walked toward a scrawny older man sitting on the couch, slowly drinking coffee. His hair was singed. One of his eyes was bandaged. His blue jumpsuit covered in burn marks. His hands shaking.

I stepped closer. "Hey, Dusty."

"Hey, Emma. I heard about your wild adventures. You guys are the talk of the station today."

"What did you get into?" I asked, gesturing toward the bandage.

"Flying fire plants. Damn do they get hot."

"Fire plants?"

"Hundreds of them." His eye widened. "Need more fire extinguishers for that zone."

"What did they look like?"

"Almost like a fish. Pinkish-orange with black speckled fins at the back, but the head was more like...almost like two flamingo heads curling toward each other, but with three eyes on each one."

Damien laughed. "We're never getting away from the flamingoes, are we? We had an anomaly cause flamingo-based dreams one night."

Dusty grinned. "Maybe we should rename this the flamingo base."

"They able to repair your ship?"

"Yeah. It'll take them a while, but it's salvageable."

"Everyone get back?"

"Yeah, surprisingly no fatalities."

"The shield didn't stop them?"

"Burned right through it. They latched onto the exterior, melting through our walls. We ended up hunkered down in the control room. Our sprinkler system helped a little...until they melted it."

"How'd you get away from them?"

"They melted through one of our core engines. Sent a shockwave through the ship. They didn't seem to like it. Flew away."

A woman with warm brown skin and curly black hair kept up in a ponytail walked in. "He telling you about the fire plant fish things?"

"Yeah," I responded. "Fuck, Gloria, I always forget how tall you are."

"Too much for you to handle, Emma?"

Damien chuckled. "Emma's currently fawning over our botanist."

"The blonde with the bird gloves?"

"Yup."

"She is pretty cute." Gloria stretched and sat down. "You'll never guess what we found before we were called to search for the *A.S.F.*"

"What?" I asked.

"*Space Whale.*"

"Seriously?"

"Owen's old ship, the one he had to abandon. Went missing years ago. We found it stuck to a meteor. Almost got stuck ourselves. Thing had a crazy magnetic pull."

"How's the ship?"

"Still in one piece. Still had its grey-blue paint job and whale-like shape. They're transporting it to Core Eight for repairs."

"Not as impressive as finding intelligent alien life," Damien said.

"But it was one hell of an adventure."

"We all had one this time," Dusty said with a smile. "This is the farthest station from Earth. The edge of the safe zone. People come out here looking for adventure."

"Definitely one of the most beautiful bases as well," Gloria added, looking out the window. "The deep blue of the Cobalt Sector to one side, and the faded red and gold of the distant Embress Galaxy at the other."

A small furry face jumped onto the couch and rubbed against my hand.

"Hey there, Moo. Follow us in here?" I asked, rubbing his back.

He meowed and headbutted my arm.

Gloria smiled. "His turn to tell adventure stories. I bet he and Milkshake were all over this station while we were gone."

Damien picked up the scrawny, mostly white cat off the floor. "If only we could see what these eyes see."

Gloria laughed. "I don't know if I want to see whatever those eyes are seeing."

"You're right. Might be better to see from Moo's perspective."

"You can. Casey put a small camera on him a few weeks ago. Those boys went into almost every room on this base in a single day. The new research cadets tracked their movements, catalogued favorite treats, and took as many funny screenshots of Commander Tills as they could. I heard that they plan on making a hilarious slide show for him if he ever transfers out or retires."

"Damn," Damien started. "I always miss out on all the fun."

"Go ask Casey to check out the footage. I'm sure they still have it."

"Where are they?"

Dusty looked toward the door. "Mechanics training, last I heard."

Damien set the cat down. "I'm off to see what secrets you fluffy boys have been hiding."

"How are you holding up, Emma?" Gloria asked. "You lost three this round."

"Had some trouble sleeping. No longer have Owen to talk me through my problems."

"Still having nightmares?"

"Rarely, when there was a lot of blood. Doesn't help that I keep injuring the same leg."

Dusty chuckled. "Maybe you should get some tattoos of protection symbols or something. Hell, tattoo a cast on it. It's been injured so many times."

"Did you go to medical yet?" Gloria asked.

"No," I responded.

She stood and pulled me off the couch. "Go on. Check in with Atla." She picked up Moo and held him in front of me. "Take this for luck so you don't break that leg again while walking down there."

I grabbed the chubby cat and smiled. "Alright. You going to lead me to medical, Milkshake?"

He meowed and peeked through the door.

Smart cat. Always knows where we need to be. Down the hallway, to the right, then the left. Upper wall stripe changes from blue to pink. Four doors down to the right, and we're standing in front of Atla's exam room. I can hear her singing...and Kenneth.

I tapped the door panel and watched it slide open. Dr. Atla stood in front of Kenneth, loudly singing along to an operatic piece.

Will I ever not see her in a ponytail? Her red hair is so curly I don't even know how she got it there in the first place.

Kenneth turned toward me and smiled. "Hey, Emma, brought our resident encouragement team?" He reached out to take Moo from me.

"Getting more opera lessons?" I asked, handing him the cat.

"I'll be great one day."

"Sure."

Atla turned the music down. "Sit on the other bed, Emma. I'm just about done with Kenneth. I got a new scanner last week that makes testing go by much faster. So far, your crew are all cleared for social interaction, nothing contagious. Kenneth and London filled me in on your creature discovery. Exciting stuff that makes me glad I refuse to touch an exploration vessel." She gestured for

Kenneth to stand. "You are free to go. Rest and make sure your sister is actually resting as well."

"Got it," he said, walking toward the door. "See you later, Emma."

Atla turned toward me and sighed. "That leg again?"

"Yes, I've already been comedically lectured by my brother and Gloria."

"Alright then, I'll spare you. Just let me adjust this scanner...hook up the blood sampler...vitals... All that looks good so far. No broken bones or missing pieces. Insides are functioning well. How's your diet been?"

"Sporadic. Missed a few meals."

"Your weight hasn't gone down too far. Exercise?"

"Only if fighting aliens counts."

"I'll count it. Anything you want to ask or mention?"

"I've been more tired lately, since I got attacked. People who physically encounter corejackers seem to feel drained afterward. Have any suggestions to counteract that?"

She reached into a nearby cabinet and grabbed a small green bottle. "Take one of these in the morning. They should help. It's a painkiller energy boost combination med. New from earth. Works wonders."

"Thanks."

Atla unhooked the scanners from my arm. "You should get some rest. Revel in the feeling of a safe bed."

"Where's the fun in that?"

"Not enough danger on the base for you?"

"I like a little excitement."

Chapter 18

Alarm's going off. Must be time to get up. Glad they gave me some time off. Sophie...in her own bed last night. Better check everyone. Where's my tablet? There... Let's see... Wait, why? Right, not on the ship anymore. Back at the station. No more daily crew readings. Honestly makes me a bit anxious not knowing how everyone is doing.

I sat up and looked at the digital panel on the wall. *Today's the day. Fuck, I don't even know if that dress still fits me. Better check... Dark blue, because of course they would prefer us color coordinate our event outfits with our section colors. At least we got over the whole wearing black for funerals thing a few decades ago. Why did they used to be so drab? I was never the best at history.*

I grabbed the dress from my closet. *Probably shouldn't put this on over my pajamas, though I bet it would be more comfortable. When was the last time I wore a dress? Must have been that last funeral a few weeks before we headed out. The* Cannon *crew, if I remember right. Lost in a solar burst. Well, it seems it still fits perfectly. Better get out there. I slept past breakfast. They'll have food after the main ceremony.*

I stretched my arms and opened the door. The familiar sounds of rubber boots against metal, electrical hums, hallway chatter, and the occasional meow from the feline brothers filled my mind with ease.

Down this hallway, left, right, down the stairs, another left, and here we are. I stared out the window at a small black ship with golden accents. *I've met the captain once before. Seemed nice, though no one really knows him. He never stays at any station for very long.*

"Wonder how haunted that one is," Sophie said, adjusting her short, dark green dress. "Ghosts hanging out together on their way back home. I almost feel like I should be sorry for them once they put our three on board. Hyke will probably rant about defense protocols. Boston would be constantly checking the ship's engine and complaining about how poorly someone put it together, and I'm sure Owen would be telling tales to any other ghosts on board."

"If Owen did end up a ghost, I doubt he'd leave this station. I can't imagine him wanting to go back to Earth, even in death. Now he gets to explore without having to worry about oxygen."

"That would make things easier. If only he could travel ahead and warn us of dangers."

"Maybe they'll come up with something to talk to ghosts in the future."

"Add a ghost comm to the ships?"

"I'm sure Hyke would torment us if we did."

Damien peeked his head through the door. "It's about to start."

We walked into a dimly lit room and sat with the rest of our crew, joining them in calm silence. The walls were covered in screens displaying images of the deceased. Three closed caskets sat against the front wall.

Commander Tills stood at the podium in a dark purple suit, contrasting his greying blonde hair. His eyes were focused; face plastered with his typical stern expression. "We mourn the loss of our people, remembering them for their bravery and strength. All of the fallen from this assignment have been retrieved. Each one fought for the safety of their crewmates, the integrity of their characters, and their devotion to exploration. We all know the dangers of the void and the risk of its adventures. Today, we wish our fallen friends safe passage on their final journey home. Robert Boston, Owen Kellner, and Mitch Hyke. Now shadows among the stars."

I can hear the tears. They always start after the names are spoken.

Tills turned and saluted the caskets, allowing for another moment of silence. "Please feel free to come up and say your final words to our fallen. When you are ready, please go into the next room for a celebration of their lives and adventures."

A few of the defense captains approached Hyke's casket, giving him one final salute.

I wonder how many of them really knew him, and how many are just here because they're also from defense. They can be rough at times, but at least they show support for their people, whether or not they knew them personally. His parents will probably brag about his sacrifice, his bravery. We all gave him shit for his punch first attitude, but he did save our asses more than once…except for Owen. I wonder if Owen's complaining to him about that right now.

Owen's casket was consistently surrounded by people from all different sectors. Old friends from his training days, new cadets he once lectured, people he laughed with, survived with, and told stories to.

Not many people knew Boston. He was one of the best engineers, but not the most social. I didn't even know him all that well. Owen said he had a wife. I wonder if she's heard the news yet. So many people don't know. Everyone back on earth has to wait for communications to pass through, like the stars in the sky that keep shining long after they have gone out because their light has to travel so far. That darkness is never instant. It takes time, and even then, only those who are looking will notice.

Emotional whispers lingered around the caskets.

Looks like most of the people have finished their goodbyes. I walked to Hyke's casket. "You were a lousy piece of shit at times, but you had good intentions. You knew weapons more than I know anything. It was annoying, and you were pushy, but sometimes I regret not listening to you. If I had been more knowledgeable in defensive and combat strategies, maybe we wouldn't have lost as many people."

The screen behind his casket shifted, showing one of the pictures he kept in his room. Hyke stood in the middle of a group of young cadets ready for training.

I turned and stepped toward Boston's casket. "Didn't have many friends, you grumpy old man? I bet they are all hiding out in their own engine rooms, mumbling complaints. Honestly, we didn't do well without you. You knew everything there is to know about engines. I preferred your honesty. You were straightforward, knew what you were saying, and got shit done. I always respected that."

His screen changed to an image of a cramped engine room with three older men sharing lunch over a small generator.

Now for Owen... I took a few steps and stared down at the glossy wooden surface. "Had enough of sad words, old man? Now I'm going to be stuck with Damien as my back up pilot. Gloria's already wished me luck with that. Going to need all I can get. Maybe you can haunt our ship and keep an eye on things for us. You always said you had no reason to go back to Earth." I paused, closing my eyes for a moment. "I miss you. Me and Damien will tell your stories, all the wild adventures you used to talk our ears off."

Sophie grabbed my hand. "I'm guessing he's not the first friend you've lost out here."

"No. Arther Clement was the first. He was my best friend. We were assigned to the same ship for our first voyage. One of the old frontier ships. Owen was the captain. We ended up getting badly damaged in a meteor ring. This was before the shield buffers. Arther was outside, trying to fix an antenna. We were barely able to retrieve him."

"I'm sorry."

Owen's voice echoed through my head. *"You can't efficient your way out of death, Emma. Arther knew that."*

"Ever failed to retrieve someone?" Sophie asked.

"A few. Thinking about being lost in the void of space doesn't really bother me, though some are unsettled by the idea."

"It would be beautiful, but pretty lonely."

"True." I stepped back and sighed. "Okay. I'm ready."

We walked into the next room, immediately met with laughter and the smell of snack foods.

"Not your typical funeral," Sophie said.

"Asrocore tries to be open about different cultural customs around death and grieving. They found that people adjust to loss better if it isn't just left in silence."

"I like it. People are having fun, smiling."

"They wouldn't have wanted it any other way."

"Even Boston? He wasn't much of a partier."

"True. He might not be having as much fun watching everyone tell embarrassing stories about him."

Commander Front turned toward us. "Like the time he accidentally attached an anti-gravity simulator to an escape pod."

"Really?"

"He originally worked for the Incipience Safety Core. The ones in charge of protecting Earth from any space-based threats. He used to be in charge of escape pod design. Back then the anti-gravity devices looked almost identical to the gravitational ones. The only difference was a thin stripe of color. He accidentally welded the wrong one onto a pod. When the ship was evacuated and people climbed in, they had trouble getting their seatbelts on."

"Not easy sitting down in zero gravity."

"Funny thing was he ended up one of the people who used that pod."

"I can picture him floating around the pod, looking completely unamused."

Sophie smiled. "I always thought space would be more professional. You guys have tons of stories of accidents and shenanigans."

"Shenanigans help lessen the stress," Front said. "Don't tell Commander Tills I said that."

"Of course."

"Are you both enjoying the festivities?"

"Still readjusting to larger crowds."

"I can give you an excuse to head out if you'd like, though it won't be a happy one."

"What is it?" I asked.

"Would you be willing to film Owen's condolence video? I know you were close. He didn't really have any family back home, so we'll be addressing the crew members he worked with, all his old friends. We were planning on sending them out tomorrow."

"I'll go ahead and start it. You want to be a part of it, Sophie? You were the last one to see him alive."

"Sure."

Front set down his glass. "The third conference hall is empty at the moment."

"Okay, we'll head there. Have fun, Commander."

"Are the condolence videos usually filmed in there?" Sophie asked, following me down the hall.

"Most of them. This room has a really good view of the Embress Galaxy. There's something comforting about the swirls of red and orange outside the window."

"They remind me of fall leaves."

I stared out at the colorful shapes. There was more orange than red, though they mixed and swirled around each other in varying shades and degrees of brightness. Bright stars flickered through the colors like tiny specks of glitter.

Sophie sat on the couch. "I've never done one of these."

"It's part of captain and commander training. I've had to do several practice videos, and an unfortunate number of real ones."

"I'm sorry."

I sat next to her and turned on the recorder. "To all crew, friends, and family of Owen Kellner. Date, November twelfth, 2193. Asrocore Base Nine, outer sector. My name is Emma Rown, captain of the *R.E.L.I-X* exploration crew.

We had quite the adventure on our first run though the Cobalt Sector. An adventure that unfortunately took the lives of several crew members. We were out exploring a new section. Several alien creatures ended up getting on board causing a power failure. Took us a few days to figure out exactly what was going on. We were able to contain the creatures to the lower part of the ship for a while. Owen was eager to help discover and neutralize our threats. You know how he was. Unfortunately, miscommunication and a door malfunction allowed the creatures to get into the lab with Owen and our lead biologist. Without him, she wouldn't have made it." I put my hand on her shoulder.

"He was kind and easy to talk to," she said. "Eliza used to get anxious about being so far away from home. He would walk into the lab, sit down, and talk with her about one of his daring adventures, how he managed to survive through tough times. It helped her calm down."

"He was one of my closest friends," I added. "Captained the first ship I was assigned to. Told stories about his countless adventures and helped guide people through their own. He was happiest in the void, jumping into the unknown. Now he can finally rest. Forever among the stars."

Chapter 19

"Uhh, Casey, why is there a sofa floating in the hallway?" I asked.

They looked back at me with wide green eyes and matching dyed hair in a messy ponytail. "Well…we thought an anti-gravity device would make it easier to move and might have gotten a bit carried away."

"Rachel helped, I'm assuming?"

"Yes."

"You two are always getting into trouble. I'm surprised you haven't been reassigned."

Casey shrugged. "Easy to get away with things as a retired captain."

"Noted."

They gestured toward the blonde woman next to me. "Who's this?"

"Sophie."

"*R.E.L.I-X* scientist, correct?"

"Yes," Sophie responded.

"I'm Captain Casey, though I don't get to pilot anymore. Had to stop after a serious collision that cost a literal arm and leg. I'm now in charge of survival training."

"What happened?"

"An unbelievably crazy series of events. You haven't heard of the *Silver Comet*'s wild adventures?"

"No."

"We were assigned to explore what we now call the mirage zone. We had no idea what we were heading into. Had about thirty people on board. Standard crew. Good people. We make it past a dense meteor ring. In front of us was a weird rippling greenish-blue mass that looked like a huge section of space ocean. We sent out a bot to get samples. It got sucked into the anomaly. The tether started slowly inching the ship closer to it. Everyone freaked out, frantically trying to release the bot. I tried to back the ship up, but the controls weren't responding. The ship started slowly creeping into the stuff. At that point we realized that we were in some sort of thick cloud of what looked like greenish colored sand. Tiny sparks started coming out of the sand particles. That's when shit got crazy."

"How crazy?"

They grinned and started moving their hands around expressively. "The gravity reversed, people were randomly floating, sparks of energy shot through the ship, and some of the crew started hallucinating. I ended up standing on the ceiling, listening to people shouting about space sharks. Rachel floated over to the control board. I had to try and explain how the controls worked while running from an imaginary space scorpion."

Sophie stared with a blank expression. "Okay...following so far."

194

"By now everyone but Rachel, General Rost, and I have completely lost it. Rost was floating around, drinking coffee, not as panicked as everyone else. He and Rachel eventually managed to get the ship turned around and started a jump sequence back to one of our map markers. The ship jumped out of there. Everyone was tossed around for a few seconds, then bam! The ship started banging into things, the emergency alarm was blaring, the shield buffer was failing, the ship was speeding through meteors, trying to auto-navigate to its destination."

"That's intense."

"I woke up a good half hour later with my right arm badly broken, left leg covered in blood. Rachel was frantically bandaging me up. Rost was trying to stabilize the controls. The ship was leaking oxygen. Half the crew had passed out. Turns out we had wandered into a breaking planet. The electricity from the thing destabilized the gravity and messed with brain waves, causing the floating and hallucinations."

"How long did this go on for?"

"A few hours. Luckily another ship was in the area. They were able to get us all back to base. The *Silver Comet* was deemed too damaged to repair. I ended up losing both limbs. Got an advanced set of custom robotic prosthetics. Rachel, Rost, and I were awarded for saving our crew, though my injuries ended up keeping me restricted to base. I still get into all sorts of trouble. Not quite as death-defying."

I spoke. "Having to emergency jump then passing out from failing said jumps seems to be a rite of passage for pilots these days."

"Right, you got knocked out jumping away from your creepy alien friends."

"I luckily got to keep all my limbs."

"So did Dusty and Gloria."

"Dusty lost an eye."

"You know that's not going to stop him from going exploring. I only had to stay because they're still working on finalizing my limb tech."

"Making those things as realistic as possible is no easy feat."

"No, but what better test than going out on another assignment?"

"I'm sure you'll have plenty of adventures here to keep you entertained. Remember the fireworks?" I asked.

"Oh, yes."

Sophie raised an eyebrow. "Fireworks?"

"I snuck a box full of fireworks onto the station for Cosmorial Day," Casey explained. "Got in big trouble with Commander Tills. I even got the fancy kind from that lab that makes safer, cleaner fireworks, and he still yelled at me about oxygen parameters for four hours."

I stepped closer. "You going to do it again? Got a surprise for us today?"

They grinned maniacally. "Perhaps..."

"Do you have any?"

"Arriving in a few minutes. Wanna join in on the fun?"

"Hell yeah."

"Let's hurry down to the supply dock, then."

Sophie smiled. "Are we about to get into trouble?"

"Only if Tills catches us," Casey responded.

"He's the always grumpy one?"

"Yes. He should be showing new recruits around right now. Shouldn't bother us."

"What about the couch?"

"Rachel's got it."

"How many fireworks do we have?" I asked, following them down the hall.

"Two crates," Casey responded. "Bonnie owed me a favor."

"Tills is going to be pissed."

"He didn't tell me not to do it again..."

Footsteps approached. Casey hid in the maintenance room.

Tills walked around the corner followed by six new cadets. "Most of the base is color-coded via the trim and doors to help define different sections and help liven up the boring grey whatever it's called that the base is made of."

"Hello, Tills," I said.

He turned toward me and stopped. "Ah, this is one of our pilots, Emma Rown, on the exploration crew. Trained under the famed Owen Kellner, and this is Sophie May, one of our biologists."

"Always glad to see new recruits. Ready for an adventure?"

"The bigger the better," one said.

"Good. We just brought in new alien lifeforms. Should give you all some fun opportunities." I stepped forward and grinned. "Just make sure you keep your flashlights on you." *Huh, now half of them look terrified. Hope they're cut out for this station.*

"Everything is perfectly safe," Tills said. "Now, let us continue. You're just in time for our Cosmorial Day dinner celebration. I know Earth has its own customs to honor our expanse into the cosmos, but out here, it is an incredibly important celebration of our unity, the amalgamation of effort and strength that allows us to be here right now, learning from the void. The farther out you get, the wilder the celebrations become, though I have a firm grasp on our station's safety regulations, so I assure you, though wonderous, it will be safe. We will head to the main dining hall next. Your training begins two days from now. Take some time to explore the station and get familiar with your new crewmates."

"Good luck." *Okay, wait for them to turn the corner, and...* "Casey, it's clear."

They stepped into the hall. "Still showing recruits around?"

"Not for long. He's leading them to the dining room."

"We'd better hurry. Bonnie said she'd meet us onboard."

"Which ship is it?"

"That copper one to the left."

A short, older woman stood by the door to the ship, watching Casey with a mischievous smile. "Larry's grabbing them for you. No one's scheduled to come by for another ten minutes."

"Thanks for letting me hide them on your ship. Tills has been extra fussy about checking every nook and cranny on this station after last year."

"Just let me know when you're going to use those things. Wouldn't want to miss it."

"We're planning to light them during the dinner celebration."

"Perfect. I'll let my crew know."

Larry walked out with two crates on a dolly. "Have fun, Casey."

They grabbed the first crate, then turned. "Can you get the second one, Emma?"

"Sure."

"We'll head through the maintenance room. Should be quicker."

"Did you disable the cameras already?" I asked, following close behind.

"Yes. They'll be back on in five minutes. Sophie, can you get the door?"

"Sure. What's the plan?"

"We still have to decide where to set them off. Probably have to do it in the void if I don't want to be yelled at again."

"How about we launch them from the P-section emergency dock?" I suggested. "It's right under that giant window."

"Great," Casey said. "How do we get there unnoticed? There are always people hanging around personnel quarters."

"Just make sure Commander Tills isn't around. The new cadets won't know anything's suspicious, and Commander Front doesn't care enough to do anything."

"Alright. Let's go."

I'm not sure how much time we have. Tills doesn't usually meander between locations. He probably led the recruits right to the room, no stops to ramble. We might not have much time. Maybe if we go through the lower maintenance section? No, too dangerous with fireworks. Carrying this box is not helping my leg. Seems like I'm ending up with permanent mobility issues. Glad we have Sophie to get the...doors...

"What's going on in here?" Tills asked, standing in the doorway.

"We're just helping Bonnie with supply distribution," I responded. "You already done with recruits?"

"I was on my way to find Casey. Commander Front mentioned that they had a training plan for corejacker encounters."

Terrible timing, Front...

He looked at Casey and frowned. "You two together, something devious must be happening."

"No, sir," Casey responded.

"What is in those crates?"

"Supplies."

"I don't see an authorization stamp on it."

"It was rushed in. You know, sometimes things run out quickly and you need to get them restocked as soon as possible."

"Put it down."

Casey set it on a bench. "Yes, sir."

Tills opened the crate. "Fireworks! Again! This is twice the amount. It isn't worth the risk. They will be disposed of immediately."

"Yes, sir."

Tills stormed out.

"Fuck."

Sophie stepped out of the corner. "Follow Tills. That way he will know you didn't do it."

"What?" Casey asked.

"He didn't see me. I'll re-hide the boxes. He won't suspect me."

"Perfect. I owe you one, Sophie."

He didn't get far. It looks like he's heading to his office. We probably should have gone a different route. Hope this plan works. Sophie's smaller than us. Hope she's able to get the crates moved without too much hassle.

"Sir," Casey started, "what if we only light a couple? Some of the smaller ones."

Tills reached for his office door. "No."

"One?"

"No."

"What if we have the scientific team analyze them first?"

"No. End of discussion. I've had enough of your dangerous stunts, Casey. Last year a tablecloth caught on fire. If it were up to me, you'd be demoted."

Casey sat down. "That had nothing to do with the fireworks. One of the defense cadets dropped a non-regulation lighter he brought out here."

Tills grabbed his phone. "Have someone remove the crates from the entrance to the first P-section hallway and take them to disposal." He turned toward me. "I'm not surprised you decided to join their mischief, Captain Rown."

"Just keeping things exciting," I said with a smile.

A chubby black and white cat jumped into Casey's lap, purring loudly.

"I bet Moo would enjoy the fireworks," they said, petting him. "He's not afraid of anything."

Tills glared down at the cat. "We have several damaged vessels and dangerous creatures contained in the R-section. No potential hazards will be tolerated. Everything must be finely assessed and controlled. We are not lollygagging around on an Earth base; we are in the void. Everything must be taken seriously."

Milkshake jumped onto his desk, waving his tail in Tills's face.

Casey chuckled. "Of course, sir. Serious..."

Tills looks completely done with our bullshit. I wouldn't be surprised if he's going to blame us for his grey hairs next.

A man walked in. "There's no crate in the P-section entrance hallway, sir."

Tills glared at Casey. "Where?"

"I don't know," Casey said. "We were here."

He sighed. "Get out of my office. If I see one firework go off in this base, I'm transferring you out."

"Yes, sir." Casey grinned and followed me out. "That went pretty well. Where do you think Sophie headed to?"

"Not sure... We were headed to the P-section docks. Let's see if she got them there." *Walk through the halls, definitely not looking suspicious...* "Casey, stop giggling."

"Right, normal day, normal activities. Nothing odd here."

"Sometimes I wonder how you get away with so much."

"There's Sophie in front of the airlock bay door."

"Everything's good," she said. "Crates are in the P-section airlock. How did it go with Tills?"

"He's upset," I responded. "Last year was kind of a mess."

Casey grinned and opened the airlock. "Only a little. No one got hurt."

I opened the first crate and picked up a small colorful tube. *Okay, Emma, be careful. Don't want anything going off in the airlock bay. Owen would love this. Sorry you aren't able to help out, old man. I wonder if you're watching us right now. This would be your ideal type of entertainment.*

Sophie stood by the door, keeping watch. "How long until you're done setting up?"

"Should only take a couple minutes," Casey answered, opening the second box. "I custom-ordered these from a friend. We just set them in these stands, set the timing fuse, light it up, and run to the dining room."

"Did you have the same stands last year?"

"Yes. My friend specially designed them for void-safe firework shows. They started having them on some of the planetary bases. Needed something to make extra sure the fireworks didn't move while being set up and lit. Asrocore stations could withstand a rocket and not get a single scratch, but it's still good to be safe."

"I'm almost done with this stand," I said, turning toward them.

"Got the fuses set," Casey said. "Three fireworks will go off every few seconds."

"Sounds good."

A fluffy critter ran in, jumping into the empty fireworks box.

Casey quickly picked him up. "Not now, Moo."

"They aren't supposed to be in here," I said, feeling something brush up against my legs. I picked up Milkshake, staring into his wide eyes. "Why do you always look like you just witnessed something crazy?" He reached his arms toward me, purring.

Sophie smiled. "He just did. Not every day someone sets up fireworks in the void."

Casey stepped closer to Sophie and held out Moo. "Hold this for me."

"With pleasure."

They walked back toward the airlock. "Okay, lighting the fuse, sending it out. It'll take a few minutes to go off. Fire doesn't work properly in the void. We should have three-ish minutes to get to the dining hall."

"Should be enough time," I said. "Luckily there aren't any checkpoints or decontamination rooms between here and there."

"For now. They add more of those each year. More people, more ships, more discoveries, more potential problems. Do we have both cats?"

"Yes."

"Let's go." Casey rushed out.

We definitely look suspicious now. Luckily everyone's already gathered. No one in the hallways to notice. I hate these stairs. We don't have time to wait for the elevator. Fuck, I'm getting more of a workout now than I got fighting aliens on the ship. There's the door... We're in.

"Why are you in such a hurry?" London asked.

"No particular reason," I said, nodding my head toward the window.

A burst of color flashed outside. Everyone turned. Milkshake jumped in my arms, staring out the window with unreasonably wide eyes. Cheering erupted. Another burst of color filled the void.

London smiled. "I heard a rumor that you were up to no good today."

Casey looked outside. "I have no idea what you're talking about."

"Well, I'm sure Moo and Milkshake didn't do this."

"No, but they did try to help."

I laughed. "Perfect crate inspectors."

Tills walked up to us, staring with an unamused expression. "Casey..."

Casey smiled. "You didn't say anything about setting them off in the void."

"No, I didn't." He sighed. "I'll let you get away with this one. I won't be so nice next time you pull a crazy stunt." He carefully grabbed the frightened cat out of my arms and walked away.

A wild grin came over Casey's face. "I'm going for a swim."

"What?"

Casey ran out the door.

Sophie walked up and handed me a soda. "Where are they going?"

"For a swim..."

"A what?"

"I don't know."

"Emma!" Gloria said with excitement. "You had something to do with this, didn't you?"

"Yes."

"I see, now that Owen isn't around to stop you, you're falling into Casey's mischievous schemes."

"They needed help carrying the second crate."

"Second crate? Going for twice the amount of last year?"

"We have twice the crew to impress. Morale is very important."

"It is...and it seems Casey is doing their absolute best to make it skyrocket."

"What?" I turned back toward the window.

Casey was floating outside in a grey void suit. Moo floated next to them in a specially tailored purple cat suit.

"Tills is going to kill them," I said.

Gloria laughed. "To be fair, Moo loves to hang around the airlock bay. Practically begs to be taken out."

Damien walked up and handed me a bowl of chips. "That idiosyncratic genius."

I smiled. "Just another day out in the void."

He paused, then laughed. "Do you think Casey knows about the glowing soap?"

Chapter 20

"Paperwork?" I asked, walking up to Casey.

They lifted their eyes from the crowded screen of a tablet. "It's not too bad this time. I was able to convince all three commanders that I can safely launch fireworks in the void."

"They're letting you do it again?"

"Every Cosmorial Day, though I have to study this new protocol, file paperwork, and properly inform them when I have a shipment coming in."

"You break the rules so hard they have to make new ones to bend around you."

"Rachel suggested making launch adaptors for ships so we can fire them into the void easier."

"Good idea. How is Rachel? I haven't seen her much since we got back."

"She's been helping plan a new ship design."

"What are they going to call this one?"

"Haven't decided yet."

Kenneth stepped into the hallway. "Hey, Emma. Front wants us to meet him in the E-section break room in ten minutes."

"Hopefully our evaluations went well."

"Do you know where Damien and London are?"

"Thought I saw them headed this way a few minutes ago."

"Hopefully they aren't far."

Casey led us down the hall and peered into the break room. "Found them." They grinned.

"What?" I asked.

"Maybe we should give them a minute, or let Front find them."

I stepped closer and opened the door. London stood right in front of Damien, glaring with mischievous eyes.

"We could do anything we want," she said. "Asrocore wouldn't know."

"Plotting to break regs?" I asked, stepping in.

Damien threw a pillow at me. "Eavesdropper."

"Don't throw things at your captain," Kenneth said, throwing it back.

Damien smiled. "It's my right as a sibling to throw what I want at her."

"I won't tolerate this kind of—" A pillow smacked into his face. "Mutiny!"

"You're not the captain."

"Right." Kenneth turned and threw the pillow at me. "Mutiny!"

I threw it back. "Traitor."

Casey stepped in between us. "Wait, hold it. There's only one way to settle this." They picked up a pillow. "War!" They threw it at Kenneth and darted behind the couch.

Fuck… Space base pillow fight, I guess.

Kenneth and London grabbed more pillows and ran for the hallway. "You, Emma Rown," Kenneth started, "shall be defeated, and we shall reign supreme as the new captains of the *R.E.L.I-X.*"

"Not if you keep throwing like a wimp," I said, dashing toward Casey. "You got more ammo?"

"A few pillows," they responded. "We can use the couch cushions after that."

Sophie walked in. "What's going on?"

"Pick a side," Kenneth said, dodging my two-pillow strike.

She ran across the room, joining us behind the couch. "I'm not the best at this..."

"Just stick with us. Where's Damien?" I asked.

"He's on their side."

"My own brother betrayed me? Villain."

Casey threw a pillow, then ducked back down. "I'll help you get revenge."

"Maybe I should replace him with you."

"Gladly. Get me off this base already."

"You're a far better pilot than him."

"Shit, they've got the bean bag pillows."

"We've still got the cushions. How about a final push?"

"I'll cover you."

I grabbed a cushion and jumped toward the hallway. Pillows flew by my face.

London jumped out and lifted a pillow. "Surrender!"

Casey jumped in front of me, tossing one toward her.

They took each other out. Now's my chance, just have to hit Kenneth... No! Damien got me, and Kenneth is going for Sophie... We've been defeated.

"Yeah!" Kenneth said, jumping up in excitement. "I am the new ruler of the *R.E.L.I-X.*"

I stopped and stared at the door. *Shit...*

Front stood behind him with an unamused expression. "I said to meet me in here, not stage a mutiny with pillows."

Kenneth jumped back. "Oh, sorry, sir. We were just settling a debate."

"Put those back and sit."

"Yes, sir."

"We're missing one."

Eliza rushed in and sat down. "Sorry, Eli wanted me to go over a report."

Front closed the door and looked down at his tablet. "I've read through all your reports. Because of your ordeal, Asrocore will require you to visit one of the onsite therapists to make sure you're cleared for further exploration. Anyone wish to go back to Earth?"

"And miss out on all this danger?" Damien said, setting down the last pillow.

"Your ship is being updated to run on inclear power. We're also making a few adjustments to your space suits. Eli is having bioluminescent fabric added to them. We're also placing rubber suits in all ships to avoid energy drain. Each ship will have two placed in the airlock bay. Any questions? No? Good. Our next topic covers Asrocore regulations, something I know a number of you have been breaking."

Pretty much all of us are guilty of that...

He glared at Damien and London. "Being your superior, I am required to tell you to stop fraternizing with your fellow crew members, though I know you're not going to listen, nor do I actually care. Moving on."

"How did you find out?" London asked.

"You're not as sneaky as you think, Miss Rail. I do talk with our security patrols. You both have been spotted on the cameras, flirting and sneaking around. As long as no one reports to Commander Tills, you should have nothing to worry about. The man's obsessed with regulations."

Damien smirked. "Just wait until we find intelligent races more like ours and have to deal with people trying to date them. Then we'd have to deal with more regulations. I'm sure Tills would be thrilled. You know they'd put him in charge of that. Then he can yell at a whole other race for breaking rules."

"Would you date an alien?" Kenneth asked.

"We've only found two kinds so far and all they want is to kill us."

"May I continue?" Front asked, glaring with unamused eyes. "We're here to discuss current events. Back to official business, Asrocore has decided to approve of a weapons system being added to your ship. We requested the engineers make it hidden so you can still appear friendly if needed."

"What type of weapons system?" London excitedly asked. "Lasers?"

"You get one laser," Front answered. "Emma and Damien will be the only ones with clearance to use them."

"Fine…"

"You will also be equipped with two manual turrets. The controls for these will be added to the control room. The laser will react to your shield barrier, so if you need to use it, you will have to remember to turn off your barrier temporarily if you don't want to electrocute your ship."

"Preferably not."

"Asrocore will be assigning a scientific crew to continue research into these creatures and their origin. Your crew will continue exploration in the Cobalt Sector with caution around their planet. We are building a new supply ship equipped with inclear power and D-Six-Zero stone plating on the sides to keep away visitors. This ship will go as far as the new D-Six-Zero station. We are oversupplying your ship so you should be good until the new one has been launched. Questions?"

"Have they released information to Earth yet?" London asked.

"Earth was informed of your initial discovery yesterday. I imagine it's all over the news by now. Asrocore still doesn't allow the press to outer stations, so you have no need to worry about being hounded for interviews. You will depart after the engineers finish adding the D-Six-Zero stone to your ship's exterior. We've uploaded your new estimated course. Any questions?"

"Can we get a vending machine?" Damien asked. "We keep running out of snacks."

"I'll think about it. Anything else?"

"What's new on Earth?" Kenneth asked.

"They've elected a new Unitatem Council representative for the U.S. Danna Plyus. Apparently used to work in the council's research department."

"Good. We seem to do better with more scientists on the council. Wonder if they released information on inclear power yet. I'm sure world leaders would be interested in bringing it to Earth."

"Tills might know. He's the most up to date on Earth's news."

"Anything else going on?"

"They're trying to get goats on Mars," Front answered. "The colonists think they'll help the natural cycle. They've been having some issues with their garden ecosystems."

"Did the council ever make up their mind about the moon base?" London asked.

"Nope, still just sitting there completely broken."

"We've had fully functional bases out in the void for decades at this point. You'd think they would be able to make one on the moon by now. Fuck, just park a large ship on it."

"They tried. It crashed into the old surface base."

"Which company tried to land it?"

"Incipience Safety Core."

"Not surprising. They're a mess. Let Casey land one. They'll get it right."

"Casey hasn't been anywhere near Earth in years."

"A true adventurer of the void."

"If you have no further questions, I'm late for another meeting. If you'll excuse me." Front nodded and walked out.

"Fuck," London said, watching most of the crew exit. "I thought the personnel hall cameras were busted."

I sat on the couch. "Just the one in hall two."

"Bet you Casey had something to do with it. They never get caught. I'm back on base for a week and I get busted for breaking regs."

"You didn't exactly get busted. How's your side?"

"Sore. Dr. Atla is having me take these weird energy pills for recovery."

"The glowing green ones that look like something out of a video game?"

"Yeah."

"She has me on the same thing."

"What is it?"

"I don't know. Sophie mentioned they had some new medical advancements while we were gone."

"Well, it definitely works better than that experimental stuff they had us try in training."

"The gooey red stuff?"

She scrunched her face. "Yeah."

"I'm so glad they stopped making it."

"I'm going to head to bed. See you tomorrow."

"Night, London."

Sophie scooted closer to me and smiled. "So, are London and Kenneth our new captains now, since they won our little battle earlier?"

"I would have gotten revenge if Front hadn't stopped us, but yeah, they won fair."

"I'm sure they'll tell stories about your tragic defeat."

"Space is full of danger."

"Who will I flirt with now?"

"Kenneth's single."

"He's not as cute as you."

"Flirting with the dead, now?"

"Just you."

"Are we going to do anything past flirting?"

"Maybe... We are alone right now." She leaned closer, gently kissing my lips.

I finally get to kiss her. If only we hadn't been fighting for our lives. I wanted to ask her out so much sooner.

The door opened. Damien stared with a wide grin.

"Now who's eavesdropping?" I said, throwing a pillow toward the door.

He ducked out of its path. "Just wanted to know if you'd gone to bed yet. Seems like you're busy. I'll see you tomorrow."

"He didn't seem too surprised," Sophie said, watching him close the door.

"Everyone's been asking me if I'd asked you out yet."

"Really?"

"What would you say if I did?"

"Yes."

Chapter 21

"Damnit!" London yelled, setting down the controller. "How are you so good at this?"

Casey smiled. "Orphans are always superior at video games."

I walked up to them. "Still losing?"

London turned toward me. "I almost had it."

"Kenneth needs your help in in the secondary electrical hub."

She stood up and glared at Casey. "I'll beat you one day."

"Doubt it," they responded, watching her leave. "What are you three up to?"

Damien lifted the flash drive in his hand. "Family response videos."

"Fun. I'll give you the room. I'm sure Tills is looking for me to do some boring lecture."

Sophie energetically walked to the screen, inserting the drive into the side.

"Snacks?" Damien asked, rummaging through the cabinet.

"I'm good," I responded, sitting down.

"Great, because they don't have any good ones."

Sophie sat next to me, excitedly grabbing the remote. "I haven't seen them in so long. I wish we could video chat with them in real time, though I understand how impossible that is way out here. It's still nice getting updates and seeing home again."

"Who do you get videos from?"

"My parents and my uncle. You'd like him. He loves space. Always excitedly talked about it when I was growing up."

Damien sat down and opened a bag of chips. "A comfortable couch, snacks, and messages from family. We're all loaded up on comfort."

Sophie started the video and put her hand on mine.

The screen lit with bright colors. Two people sat on a light blue couch. A shorter woman with long, golden wavy hair and a taller bald man with a short brown beard.

"My parents," Sophie said with a smile. "Danna and Otto."

"Hey, Sophie," Otto said. "We're all doing well. Hope you're having fun out there."

"Of course she is," a man said from behind the camera. "Can't imagine what sort of alien plants she's discovered so far."

"That's my Uncle Tom," Sophie explained. "He always sounds excited."

The camera turned around, showing Tom's face. He had light golden hair and bright blue eyes. "I've been trying to convince your younger cousins to sign up for one of the space programs. They're too nervous."

"You try to convince everyone to go to space," Danna said.

"It's a great career."

"Dangerous."

"Only a little."

"She mentioned being assigned to the farthest station; exploring the unknown is more than a little dangerous."

"She's on one of the most updated ships there is. The Research Exploration Laboratory Intelligence, type X. I'm sure she's having a blast!"

Her father looked out the window. "It's been snowing for a week straight. Nothing too wild. Soft and slow flakes. Mild wind. Absolutely beautiful."

I haven't seen snow in so long. Haven't even thought about the weather, the warmth of the sun, the ice covering the lake in the winter. Every day is pretty much the same out here. Consistent temperatures and automatic day-night cycles. In some ways, Earth is just as wild and unpredictable as the void.

"Maybe we should send you a video of the snowfall," Otto continued.

They talked for a while about the changing seasons, new fencing along their driveway, newly elected state representatives, new nieces and nephews, and updates on old friends.

I'd watch the news more often if these three told it all. Not sure if that's because they have a great dynamic, or I've just been out here so long, any news is welcome. Spending the last however many days it's been just trying to survive made all the simple things much more of a delight. No one's fighting back on earth, no news of terror and death, just medical advancements, funny pet videos, and local gossip.

"We have an update on the pair of northern cardinals," Otto said. "Looks like Cherry's wing is better. They've been whirling around the yard all day. You might see them fly by the window every now and then."

"Oh!" Her mother's expression shifted with excitement. "Your uncle and I saw a snowy owl just the other day. We agreed to name him Sir Wintersworth. He has one solid black feather at the end of his tail that makes him easy to spot. I wonder if he'll still be around next time you're home."

"I took some marvelous pictures of him," Tom added. "I'll add them to the file."

"We should let you get back to your discoveries," Danna said, grabbing her husband's hand. "I'll keep an eye on our new friend. Perhaps I can get your aunt to come out and draw him soon."

"Don't stay away too long," her dad said. "Love you. Hope those space plants aren't being too difficult."

Tom turned the camera around and waved. "Felis regere universum."

I turned and smiled at Sophie. "Of course you name the birds living around your house."

"We have seven regulars and fourteen that come and go seasonally. I'm excited to see the new snowy owl."

221

"Sir Wintersworth is a pretty great name."

"Tom always comes up with good ones."

"I think there was a pair of robins that lived near our house. Dad liked to try and hold out some seeds as still as he could to see if they'd land on him. I remember when he held still for a full twenty minutes, and a different bird jumped onto his hand and grabbed a beak full of seeds. Flew away so fast I couldn't even tell you what exactly it looked like. Dark brown, maybe black? Too quick to tell."

"Do you have a video too?"

"Yeah, from our dad," Damien said, grabbing the remote. "We never named any birds, but my friends and I named a pair of squirrels that liked to hang out on our mailbox. Tip and Tap. Loudest and bravest squirrels in the area."

A simple old cabin appeared on the screen.

"Looks like he got the windows repainted," Damien said. "They almost look out of place against the old exterior paint."

Dad sat on the porch with his usual blue cap covering his unruly dark hair and a smile plastered on his wrinkly face.

His eyes get greyer every year. Hope they still aren't hurting him. The doctor said they might eventually.

"Hey kids. Hope everything's going alright with your new ship. Couldn't stop laughing after your last recording. Hope I get to meet Captain Casey one of these days. You two seem to be having too much fun out there." He chuckled. "Your package got here. Damn those jumpsuits of yours are comfortable. Fell asleep on the couch in it yesterday."

Sophie glared at me. "Sent your dad a suit?"

"One of the spare cadet ones. No one will miss it."

"Everything's going good back here," dad continued. "Old Bob's been helping me fix up the house. He's retired now."

Bob walked into view, waving at the camera. He was an older man with short grey hair, a tattered old cowboy hat on his head, and a big friendly smile on his face. "Don't be getting into too much trouble out there, you two," he said.

"He keeps trying to talk me into getting a seeing eye dog," my dad continued, "or one of those assistant dog bots your company makes. I'm doing fine on my own."

"You'd be doing great if you had one," Bob said, glaring at him. "Won't be so lonely, either."

"Says the man who's lived alone for the last forty years."

"I like the peace and quiet."

"You aren't quiet."

Bob got out a guitar and sat next to dad. "I like it when other people are quiet."

"You going to sing them that new song of yours?"

Bob strummed his guitar. "Old man on a porch, sitting all alone. His kids are in space, can't call on the phone. Waiting and waiting to hear about their travels, while his old brain rattles and unravels. Old man on a porch, sitting alone. His sanity depleting, his beard overgrown." He laughed.

"My beard is fine."

"It's beyond fine, at this point it could be its own state."

"Emma was talking about a mustache competition between some of her coworkers. They'd respect it better than you do."

"I respect it, you just need to tame it a little. Too scraggly right now, right, kids?" Bob glanced at the camera. "Just let Rhonda trim it for you. You trust her more than me."

"You sing off-key songs about me. Lies are all I hear."

"What lies?"

"My brain isn't unraveling. I'm still sharp as ever and I'm not lonely. You can't handle a day without seeing me. Rhonda has to drag you off my property half the time."

"I'm the helpful type."

Dad shook his head. "Anyways, your uncle stopped by last week to say hi. Still working on the same train. You're friends Porter and Crystal got married. Had the celebration in that old exploration vessel that's now a museum. The *Fox*...something."

"*Fox Freighter*," Bob added.

"Right. They got a couple cardboard cutouts of you two and took a bunch of ridiculous pictures of them."

Bob laughed. "Damien's caught the bouquet! Got stuck perfectly on your head. It was wild."

"Fuck," Damien said, looking at me. "Now I have to get married."

Dad held out a hand. "That camera's waterproof, right?"

"Yeah," Bob responded.

Dad turned back toward the camera. "It's raining again. Let me know how things go with Sophie. Me and Bob got a bet going. I'd better get inside before it starts pouring. You know how the weather is out here. Later, kids."

The TV went black.

"Is that where you lived?" Sophie asked.

"Yeah," I responded. "We didn't have much. Dad couldn't work after he lost his sight. He was so proud when Damien and I were accepted by the Asrocore Pilot Academy."

"What happened to him?"

"The scars on his face?"

"Yes."

Damien took my hand and gave me a reassuring smile. "Me, Emma, and our older cousin Dale were out in the woods, climbing trees, having fun. Mom and Dad were by the lake. Just a typical Saturday at first."

"How old were you?"

"Emma was twelve. I was fourteen. Dale was...sixteen, I think." He paused and took a breath. "A storm hit. Emma fell out of the tree, broke her leg. Dad rushed over to get her. The four of us hurried back to the house. I stayed with Emma. Dad and Dale went out to find Mom, then the power went out. The house was getting thrashed with crazy winds, rain, lightning. I did my best to wrap up her leg, but I wasn't exactly that well-trained in first aid as a teen."

"You did pretty good, honestly," I said.

"We waited for about a half hour," he continued. "Made jokes to drown out the anxiety. Finally saw a figure dragging another toward the house. It was Dale and Dad, soaking wet, covered in blood. They had found our mother trying to re-secure the boat. One of the trees fell onto the dock." He paused again and squeezed my hand. "Dale had to drag them out of the water. Mom didn't end up making it."

I stared out the window, remembering the rain tapping on my skin, the wind picking up. *The tree...the blood...*

Sophie put her arm around me. "You okay?"

"Yeah. It...still gets to me sometimes. Dad started making rules for every potentially dangerous activity after that. Something to help all of us feel a little better. Rules for storms, power outages, car accidents, anything that could do harm. That's why Damien and I are always talking about step three."

Damien crossed his arms and glared at me. "How many times have you broken that leg?"

"I didn't break it this time!"

He smiled, then looked at Sophie. "She broke it again a few years later trying to jump off the roof in a hurry when our dad got home. We were supposed to be in bed. Then she broke it during combat training our first year at Asrocore."

Sophie gently placed her hand on my leg. "Maybe you should be a little more careful."

Damien smiled. "A lot has happened since our last video. Why don't we send him an update? Old Bob comes by to watch them with him, explain some of the visuals."

"Does your dad not want prosthetics?"

"No. He said he'd rather live the rest of his life blind than never see his wife again. Still says good morning to her, even though he knows she's gone."

"That's sweet."

"I'm sure he'll love to hear from you, Sophie. Emma couldn't stop talking about you in our last video."

I glared at him. "You going to tell him about London?"

"We're not dating..."

"Officially. You know he won't care about Asrocore regs."

"Okay, okay." He clicked the remote. "Hey Dad, good to see you."

"Loved the song, Bob," I said. "Miss hanging around the campfire listening to you and Rhonda singing, having a good time. Hope she's doing well."

"We've had quite a few adventures since our last recording. Emma hurt her leg again. Surprising, I know. I'm sure you'll hear about it on the news soon. We ended up getting invaded by an alien race. We didn't even know they were on our ship at first. Crazy looking things. Stand on two legs, short, thick tail, arms with one long, thick finger and a curvy, pointy thumb. Pointed faces with no mouth. Dark eyes, thin tendrils attached to their backs that wave around. A few spikes on their backs as well. Dark, oily colored skin."

"Quiet creatures that absorb energy and hate the light," I added. "Crazy strong, like broke open a barred door strong. They bent it like a paperclip, and they can take bullets like it's nothing but a weak punch. They snuck on from another ship, smart enough to hide and wait for a good opportunity. They like to sneak around and strike fast. Ended up losing a few of our crew."

"We're doing alright now. Found a way to contain them, found the other ship. Research is having a field day."

"Eli hasn't slept a wink."

"Still following your rules," Damien continued. "Currently back on base, relaxing and enjoying not fighting for our lives. Sophie's with us."

"Hello," she said.

"She's Emma's girlfriend now. Old Bob owes you ten bucks." He looked at Sophie. "They always bet ten bucks."

"Any particular reason?" she asked.

"Not that I know of," I responded, looking back at the TV. "Damien's not exactly lonely either."

He smiled. "Yeah, well...I've started seeing someone. Officially it's against the rules. You know how Asrocore is. Her name's London. We've told you about her before. She's our programmer. Really smart. I think you'd like her."

"He'd probably like me more," Kenneth said, walking in.

"That's her twin brother, Kenneth. Don't mind him, he's just sour because he's single." Damien turned toward him. "What's up?"

"Emma has been requested in the training department. Front wants her to lecture a class on surviving an encounter with corejackers."

Damein stood up. "This should be fun."

I turned back toward the camera. "Gotta go, Dad. Time to lecture new recruits about step three."

"Have you ever done a lecture before?" Sophie asked, following us out.

"Nope. Shouldn't be too hard, Owen used to do them all the time. He said that they get boring after a while. Same words, different ears. New faces all with their own levels of excitement and anxiety." *Let's see, looks like we're going into lecture hall-B today. Did they ever fix the chairs in A? Casey is standing by the entrance.* "Of course you're here."

"Wouldn't miss this for anything," they said.

I stepped in and looked over the crowd of new cadets. *Okay, look stern but not aggressive, just like Owen said. Don't let them talk over you. Keep it short and direct.*

Damien smiled and gave me a thumbs up.

"Space is serious," I started. "It may not seem that way at times, but one moment of error, one second of lost focus, and death will leap out at you before you have time to react. My crew's last mission involved exploration into the

Cobalt Sector. Everything was calm and quiet for the most part, minor anomalies and a few new situations we had to adjust to. Most of what you'll be doing is adjusting, adapting, and learning. You need to know your ship, your crew, and have an open mind." *I remember sitting in those chairs, listening to Owen give this speech. It feels so different being on the other side of the room.*

A few excited faces nodded, whispering among themselves.

"During our venture, we encountered an alien race," I continued. "Recently classified as RiorBlue lifeforms. We nicknamed them corejackers. They are intelligent and hostile. The creatures were able to hide on our ship for several days before our power went out and people started getting attacked. These lifeforms are able to absorb energy both mechanical and biological. Luckily, they fear light. We were able to use new inclear tech to deter them enough to set up a plan for their capture. We had to learn new methods of safety, and fight for our lives against intelligent creatures."

"Do we know how intelligent?" one cadet asked.

"Smart enough to figure out how to sabotage the doors. I'm sure our research department will give more information soon. You are allowed to go and visit their facility and ask more specific questions about the lifeforms."

"Do we know how to fight them?"

"To ensure we do not have any further problems with these creatures, we are now implementing inclear devices on all exploration vessels, as well as improved wire coating and power saving technology. This will help you stay safe, but it will not be enough. These things don't make sound, they don't have a strong scent, and they blend into the shadows. They are capable of handling several gunshot wounds before going down. Those of you trained in combat will be assigned new inclear weaponry. All personnel regardless of station will be given updated jumpsuits. Do not try to use limited energy-based tools to fight them. Avoid physical contact and do daily checks of all rooms and stations. Never assume all cameras and sensors are accurate. Any questions?"

A younger gal raised her hand. "What do they usually do to take us down?"

"They tear into flesh with large, bony, clawlike structures to quickly take out prey. They have the advantage of camouflage in dark areas, so be aware of your surroundings."

A man stood. "I heard there were several on the ship. Do they work as a team?"

"Yes, efficiently. Two were able to distract our defense expert, while another snuck past and attacked some of our crew." *Some of them look scared now. I can't blame them. If they saw what those things did to Owen... His chest... The blood... Shake it off, Emma. Got to finish this lecture. Don't let them see the fear. Experienced eyes need to show confidence.*

"Do we know where we should aim our weapons? Head? Chest?"

"Not yet. Further detailed information will be provided by our lead scientist, Eli Capsotters. He has been working with my own crew's scientific research team. Even with all these lectures, you need to know that this is dangerous. You might die, but you probably won't. Don't let that deter you. This is an opportunity to see the universe, to expand humanity. Fear can be overcome. May you find your own adventures out there." I smiled and walked out. *Fuck, that was stressful...*

"Thief," Damein said, nudging my shoulder.

"Those closing words worked on us."

"I'm sure Dad will love this."

"That why you were recording?"

"That and maybe future blackmail."

I shoved him into the wall. "I still have those pictures."

"Then we're even."

"Pictures?" Casey asked.

"Nothing." Damien looked back into the lecture room. "Wonder if any of them got stuck with their siblings as well. Think they're ready?"

"Ready enough," I responded. "Of course this has to be my job now."

"I'm sure Owen appreciates not having to do it anymore."

"I get why he hated it so much. So many new eyes, all waiting for me to say something inspirational or give them the key to success."

"Some of them seemed enthusiastic."

"Yeah, but the two in the back looked like they were going to pass out from stress when I was talking about how easy it is to die out here."

"Makes it more fun, like a challenge. See who can live the longest. I bet it's going to be the one in the middle who didn't say anything. They seem smart."

Casey's expression grew glum as they looked over the crowd.

"You okay?" I asked.

"I had my best friend with me all through training. Her name was Charlotte Grace. We were both a little nervous when we got our first assignment in the void. Spent a night staring out at the stars, trying to convince ourselves that it would be fine. My comedic ass of course had to turn it into a bet. Whoever lived longer got to choose what the other had on their grave marker."

"I like that bet," Damien said, glaring at me. "I think I'd put, Emma, breaker of many legs, always her own."

Casey closed their eyes and sighed. "After that night, we were no longer afraid. We had each other and just enough competitiveness between us to make every adventure fun. Neither of us wanted to lose."

"What happened?"

"She ended up getting assigned to help launch a new station. Smaller one out in sector 830-P-8."

"The *Eighth Eagle*?"

"Yeah."

"Oh, I'm sorry."

"I was still at the main base helping Gloria with new ship inspections. We'd only been apart for a day when it happened. I took the next ship I could out toward where the *Eighth* was last seen. Saw chunks of metal floating around and a badly damaged ship that was supposed to be docked at the station, but no sign of the *Eighth* itself and no survivors." They let out a sad chuckle. "I don't even know if I won or not. She could still be out there, maybe even hanging out with her own alien friends."

I put a hand on their shoulder. "It wouldn't surprise me with all the life we're running into out here."

"Sucks not knowing if she's okay. Most likely not."

"If she's as stubborn and troublesome as you, I'm sure she's alive purely out of spite."

They laughed. "Thanks."

Chapter 22

I never get tired of this. The scientists are so lucky to get a full dome view of the stars all day, every day. Brand new research section. Everything is shiny and clean. Perfect for those space career commercials Damien and I used to watch growing up. It has all the latest tech to intrigue people into joining up.

Sophie led me toward a smaller black dome in the center of the room, surrounded by research stations and equipment.

Eli walked up to us wearing his heavily stained green jumpsuit, missing half of the flask surrounded by DNA logo on the chest. "Welcome back. We have infra-red cameras hooked up to inclear power. This way we can monitor the creatures and keep them alive with the same system. We've had nonstop visitors for the past few days. Everyone wants a look. There's even a poll going on what to name them."

"What are the current favorites?" Sophie asked.

"Trident, for the big one with only three spikes on its back. Arrow for the dark one, and Shield for the injured one, since it likes to protect the others. People also suggested Creepy, Scary, and Spooky. Several different languages words for Shadow, Oil, and Blue. My assistant suggested Al, Eye, and En."

I smirked. "Alien? Pretty good."

"How much energy do they need to live?" Sophie asked.

"Not much if they're healthy. We offered more to the injured one. The more energy we gave it, the better it did. Still needed time to recover."

"Do you have them separated?" I asked.

"We did at first so we could have better access to the injured one. We have them all together currently. The other two kept pacing the wall, investigating it. They're clearly social creatures."

"We did see them in groups at the planetary collision."

"Arnie found two dead ones in the *A.S.F.* Both were riddled with bullets and knife wounds. They are incredibly resilient creatures."

"No other ships interacted with the *A.S.F* before the *Tugboat* got there?"

"Not that I know of. All other ships in the area have been updated on the situation. The damage on the side of the *A.S.F* looked similar to the shape of the larger creatures' claws. There's a possibility they moved it closer to their territory."

"The *Vision Three* was also pretty far into the meteor ring. Had the same markings on the side."

"I wonder if they intended that," he said. "If they are intelligent enough to lure prey closer to them."

"How would they know there were more of us to lure?"

"I don't know," he responded. "I would believe if I found a living creature out in space, that there would be more somewhere."

I stepped closer to the dome. "I wonder exactly how intelligent the bigger ones are compared to our guests here."

"I'll have my team analyze the footage further. We'll keep you updated."

"Thanks, Eli."

"We do know that the corejackers have to touch things to drain power. Their hands and the thin waving structures on their backs are lined with energy absorbing cells. I'd imagine the same rule applies to the larger ones as well."

"I don't remember them touching our guns. Mine and Owen's lost power when we were looking around."

"One quick tap with a tendril will do. They absorb fast."

"How about other functions?"

"They don't have any sort of digestive or respiratory systems, which isn't too surprising. Their bones and muscles are fairly dense, more so than I predicted."

"What about these dark blue structures running down their bodies?"

"I believe that's what they use to get the energy to their bloodstream. They don't have a heart. We believe their blood vessels are lined with energized cells to keep their blood moving."

"So, they're smart and well built?"

"Yes, though we're still not sure how they could survive the destruction of their planet. The tests we've run do confirm that they inhabited it before it broke apart."

"Could it have broken apart slowly?"

"Possibly. We're still analyzing some of the finer elements that make up the rock samples. It could simply be something we don't understand yet."

"Always a ton of that in space."

"And we get to be the ones discovering it. Are you heading back out today?"

"Yeah, they're having us escort the new pre-station to the D-Six-Zero anomaly. After that, we're traveling past the corejacker planet."

"Sounds terrifying. I'm glad to stay here, sleep in safety." He picked up his tablet, looking through a new report. "Speaking of sleep, just got the results back from the wave scanner. Our friends only sleep when injured or low on energy. They don't have as many organ systems to support. All they need is enough energy to maintain blood flow, muscle, brain, and bone."

"Good to know. I'll let you get back to work. We'll bring you back something cool next time we visit."

He smiled. "You always do. Arnie wanted to speak with you. He said he would meet you at the dock."

"I'll find him."

Sophie followed me out. "I'm going to check on the new base garden one more time before we leave."

"How are the new plants doing?"

"Wonderfully. Even Tills was impressed by my work."

"You are brilliant." I gave her a kiss, then turned down a different hall. "See you on board." *I wonder how the retrieval of the supply ship went. Didn't know they would be back today, though I'm glad they arrived before we had to leave. We need all the information we can get. Ah, there he is. Scraggly red head with a pristinely clean blue jumpsuit.*

"Emma, you look good. Everything alright?" Arnie asked.

"Just catching up with Eli about our alien friends," I responded.

"Really?" He turned toward a group of new cadets.

"Yeah." I smirked. "Did you guys hear about that? Had to fight a bunch of aliens using flashlights and rocks."

"Rocks?" a cadet asked.

"Space is strange."

"Very," Arnie agreed.

I turned toward him. "How'd it go?"

"Surprisingly well. No living creatures. Two dead corejackers. Looked like they took a hell of a lot of bullets to take down."

"Not surprising. The one we injured took multiple rounds from Hyke's experimental rifle."

"We were able to recover all of the bodies. At least these creatures leave us bodies to identify and retrieve. The funeral will be held tomorrow."

"See any of the big ones?"

"Nope. What did they look like again?"

"About the size of a bus. Long body, big arms, three tails, and no eyes. Creepy stuff." I smiled at the cadets.

"Is that a standard mission?" a smaller man asked.

I looked toward the docked ships, staring at the heavily damaged *Wandering Eagle.* "Yeah, pretty much. Nothing better than a good fight with an alien race to make you feel alive."

Commander Front walked in. "Alright, cadets. It's getting late. Get some rest." He looked at Arnie and me. "Trying to scare them off again?"

Arnie grinned. "No."

"Get to the platform, Emma."

"Yes, sir."

Arnie waved. "Have fun."

Hope I can this time. It would be nice to explore without fatalities. Wonder what the ship looks like now. Kenneth said something about new paint in a few rooms. Hope they didn't go too obnoxious with the colors.

"Just in time," Damien said, watching me race up the ramp and join him in line.

Front stepped onto the platform with a stern look on his face. "Your ship has been refitted for inclear power. Doors and emergency protocols have been updated. All damage repaired. The Cobalt Sector has been deemed a restricted zone. Only assigned inclear ships are permitted entry. You will be sent out to test the new power and security systems. If everything checks out, you can continue your exploration. Any questions?"

"Can we go now?" Damien asked.

"Itching to leave the station, Navigator Rown?"

"Itching to get away from question-hungry cadets and Tills's angry stares."

"Fair enough. Go ahead."

I stepped onto the ship and looked around. "I'm going to go check out our new power systems. You make sure control is good."

"Of course, Captain," Damien responded.

Wow, the ship looks good as new, no more bullet holes or stains. Looks like they adjusted the wall colors a little, nothing drastic, still grey and blue. They also added glowing stripes along the floor for emergencies. Similar aqua color the bio panels emit. That'll make things easier next time we find something wild, unless we come across an alien race that finds lights offensive. Then we're screwed. Enough thinking like Damien. Let's see what the new inclear power looks like.

A faint orange glow emerged from the power room. Two large, glowing clear tubes ran vertical against the back wall. Between them was a black power box covered in switches.

"Looks cool," I said, stepping closer.

Sophie walked in. "The tubes are filled with different compounds found in the Embress Galaxy. Keeping them close together creates an infinite supply of energy."

"What happens if the compounds mix?"

"They just stop glowing. It's surprisingly safe."

"Good. Did they adjust the oxygen sensors?"

"Yes. My plants have grown significantly over the past couple weeks. We shouldn't even need the oxygen converter for the most part."

I turned toward one of the pots by the door. Its vines wrapped up around the frame, covered in circular aqua leaves. "Yeah, those things are a lot bigger. Has anyone tried them yet?"

"One of the station chefs tried them in a few different recipes. The bluer ones are a bit sweeter, like yams, and the greener ones are more like a cross between eggplant and zucchini. The tomato plants didn't change as much. Brighter color, same flavor, but now much more durable."

"Interesting."

"They left us a few recipes and a note saying not to let London cook it by herself."

"Smart."

"I should go to the lab and get ready for launch."

"Bring your cozy pajamas again?"

"Yes."

"Why don't we have a movie night while we're heading back out? It should only take a few days to get back now that the dash systems work."

"Did we get popcorn?"

"Damien made sure to grab a few extra boxes before boarding."

"Perfect." She leaned in for a kiss. "You might want to get to control before Damien tries to pilot us out of here."

"That wouldn't be ideal." I turned toward the stairs. *This area looks good as well. Couldn't even count how many bullet holes and blood splatters were here earlier. The storage room is clean too... Hyke... I should have listened to him more. He didn't know those things were that smart.*

"We didn't end up getting the vending machine," Damien said, watching me walk into control. "Though we were able to get our hands on an extra cargo box filled with snacks, courtesy of Casey."

"Casey is the best." I sat down and grabbed the controls. "Ready?"

"Ready."

"Let's get going. I'm tired of being on base."

"Not enough drama for you?"

"I hate doing lectures."

"Understandable."

"Let's start slow, test the new inclear charge. Power is at one hundred percent. Shouldn't go down even if we run into more corejackers."

"With our current luck, we'll run into something else we're not prepared for."

"Like light-seeking aliens."

"Or ones that find lights offensive," Damien suggested.

"I was thinking that exact thing when I saw the glowing floor stripes."

"It'll be much harder to sneak around the ship at lights out."

"What reasons do you need to sneak around for?"

"Nothing in particular…"

I looked down at the control panel. "Everything's running smooth. Hitting the release." *We seem to be floating nicely. Should be far enough from the docks in three…two…one…*

The ship jerked suddenly.

"And you won't let me drive?" Damien said, glaring at me.

"Shit. Sorry. The power increase is making the controls more sensitive."

"We should have done a test flight before heading out." He tapped the comm. "We're mobile, Gloria."

The *E.E.E* sat in the distance. "Mobile as well, *R.E.L.I-X*. Lead the way."

"Glad we have an escort this time."

"Only for our systems check. We'll split off to search another zone once we reach the collision site you found."

"It'll be nice getting to chat. I'm sure you enjoy being back on exploration instead of defense training."

"Couldn't wait to get back out. Plus, I have a friend on board who's been itching to explore…"

Damien raised an eyebrow. "That sounded suspicious."

"Want to say hello?" Gloria asked.

"Sure…"

"Hey, Rown siblings."

"Casey?" Damien smiled. "What the hell are you doing on the *E.E.E*? I thought you weren't allowed to leave base?"

"Gloria thought I could use some air."

"Technically there's less air on ships, but okay. You're going to get thrown into the void for this."

"Commander Front won't care, and I'm sure Tills will be happy I'm not on base causing mischief. I'm just giving him a vacation."

"He'll need it after your stunt on Cosmorial Day."

"He won't have to see another firework until I get back."

"And what exactly do you mean by that?"

"Well, Bonnie said I deserve a celebration if I come back to base in one piece this time. She might be getting me another special shipment."

Damien shook his head. "Damn, Casey, you know how to live."

"If I had to do one more lecture, I would have set fireworks off in Tills's office. Besides, I've already survived one crazy space anomaly. What's a few more?"

"You've only got two more limbs to lose."

"I'm keeping those on this time, thank you."

"You and Gloria on a ship together. I can't even imagine the shenanigans you two will get up to."

"We've also got Rachel, Rost, and Dusty."

"Dusty? He cleared for void travel?"

"No, but you know him. He can't stand being on a base for more than a couple weeks."

"None of you can. Fuck, we're going to have to step up our game if we're having to compete with your crew. You have too many wild cards on board."

"First one who finds the next anomaly gets to light the fireworks next year."

I smiled. "Well, you'd better get planning on how you're going to beat us. Our ship is faster than yours now."

"Yeah, but you all have better sleep schedules than us. You know Gloria spends way too much time in the control room, and I can't remember the last time I saw Dusty get more than five hours of sleep a night."

"He's crazy."

"Crazy gets him through dangerous situations."

"Can't argue with that."

Chapter 23

I walked into the break room, grabbing a slice of pizza.

"Are we getting close?" Eliza asked.

"Should be there soon," I responded.

"I feel a lot safer having another ship around. How long are they going to follow us?"

"We'll split after we reach the collision planets."

"I still think they should send exploration ships out in pairs."

"Would be safer but less efficient. Doubling up exploration routes would mean half the coverage. Takes a long time to get proper void exploration ships built. It's also harder to keep larger numbers of people alive in emergency situations than just a few."

"Yeah, I guess you're right, but I still think we should be more careful. We weren't prepared to handle the corejackers."

"Space isn't predictable. There's no way to know what we're going to run into out here. We just have to adapt to whatever comes our way."

"At least we know more about those creatures."

She looks tired. Still isn't getting proper sleep. I stepped closer. "If you need someone to talk to, you can come to me. I don't have a psych degree, but I've been through enough to understand the stress."

"Thanks. I'm sure I'll feel better when we get this new repellent plating tested. I know it works; I helped discover the science behind it. I just need to see it in action."

"That's fair. If you need any extra stress relief, you can always grab a mop handle and practice combat with Kenneth. I'm sure you'd be able to kick his ass."

She smiled. "I guess I should learn more of that now that we're lacking a defense expert. Why didn't they reassign us new crew?"

"Didn't have enough. We lost all crew from the *Vision Three* and *A.S.F.* Most new recruits are going to be assigned to supply. You have more than enough medic training, and Kenneth spent the last couple weeks helping the station crew install the new inclear power, so he knows our core engines inside and out."

"Right."

"We should get more crew next time we check in at base. Tills has a whole new group of fresh cadets ready for training. They'll be able to learn about our corejackers before being sent out."

"Good."

"Looks like we're about there," I said, turning toward the door. "Get ready for the safety evaluation." *We'd better not lose power again. All this fancy new tech needs to work this time.*

"Welcome back," Damien said, watching me walk into control.

"Any movement on the scanners?"

"Not yet."

"I'll maneuver us around the edge of the meteors. We should make sure our new D-Six-Zero plating works." I grabbed the comm. "Come in, *E.E.E.* We're approaching the collision. Everyone, keep your eyes peeled for movement."

Damien sat down. "Strange how dark it all is. All these chunks are either black or dark brown. Most other structures we've found out here have had some sort of blue coloration."

"A void within the void. What's the scanner say? No gravity. Weird for such a large planet."

"Space is strange."

"There, to the right. Two corejackers on that rock, staring at us."

He looked up at the looming shadows. "Seems good so far. They aren't approaching."

"See any phantomjacks?"

"There are a few on the movement scanner. They seem to be staying closer to the planet. Don't know if they can see us. Did Eli ever mention what exactly they can see?"

"He believes they see energy levels, kind of like how a snake sees heat."

"So, we probably look like a large, glowing object."

"Most likely."

"I wonder how they survive out here. I don't see anything nearby that they can absorb energy from unless they just hunt each other."

"Maybe there are other creatures we haven't seen yet. Anything could be hiding in the rocks or on what's left of the planet, or maybe the energy they got from its destruction was enough to keep them going for a while."

"The phantomjacks are clearly able to travel through the void on their own. Maybe they go out looking for energy to bring back for the rest. They did drag two ships out here."

"I set the autopilot to hover."

Damien leaned back in his chair. "Kinda wish we could stick around for a while, study them a little more."

"Asrocore wants us to check for other life forms in the area. There might be more creatures that came off that planet that just didn't stick around. They want to make sure the new station is safe. Besides, I don't think Eliza would be fond of the idea of staying in an area that's literally surrounded by aliens. She already has trouble getting enough sleep."

He pointed to the left. "Damn, that's a big phantomjack. Almost double the size of the first two we saw."

"Wow. It's covered in scars. Its right arm is missing. A large chunk of rock stuck in its side. Looks like it's been though a lot. These things can really take a beating."

"Maybe it's one of the ones that survived the collision. Looks pretty old... Kind of reminds me of Dad with that big scar on its face."

I looked at him with a smile. "Old Daniel?"

"Perfect name. Dad would love it."

"Are we getting any sound from Old Daniel?"

Damien flipped a switch. "None."

"Makes me feel like we're in a creepy silent film."

"It's getting closer. Let's see what the panels do."

The creature shifted its head.

I leaned closer. "Looks like it's analyzing us, showing caution. Not as bold as the first two."

A small, blue electric shock sparked between its arm and our ship.

"It didn't like that," Casey said over the comm. "Wonder what it feels like to them."

"Probably like when you hit a nerve, you know," I responded. "Sudden electrical shock, kind of feeling."

"It's not acting aggressively so far."

"Keep some distance, just in case."

"I wonder what it's thinking."

"Probably wondering what the fuck we are and why it can't absorb us."

"Nothing's getting too close to our ship. Had a good-sized group of corejackers approach our side, but they all ran back after getting shocked. We are untouchable."

"Only for these things. How long do you want to stay?" I asked.

"We'll hang out for a while, get a more detailed map scan of the area and send data to the new base crew," Casey answered. "You can head out to your new section if you'd like. Ready to get back to exploring?"

"Ready. These stars are starting to look too familiar."

"Don't hog all the fun."

"I'll make sure to leave you some anomalies. Nice dangerous ones. I know how you like them."

"I've got to get as many good stories as I can. Got to impress Charlotte when we find her."

"Leaving formation. Good luck, Casey."

"Luck to you, Rown siblings. Let's see who can find the next alien race first."

"Challenge accepted."

"Think they'll be okay?" Damien asked.

"They have Gloria, Rachel, and Dusty aboard. Those four could probably survive a black hole. They'll be fine."

"Now we head back to the unknown."

"Autopilot is active. Keep an eye out. We don't know if the corejackers are capable of traveling through space or just on objects."

"Would be pretty unsettling finding one floating through space."

"Let's hope we don't."

"Would we just leave it or should we try to help it? I mean, we do have containment for them. Maybe we could make friends. At least tether it and drag it back to a rock."

"We'll figure that out if we actually find one. Let's try not to get attacked this time."

"Where's the fun in that?" He smirked. "How big is our new zone?"

"Twice the size. We have to make up for the loss of the *Vision*."

"Good. Let's get lost." He reached for his mug.

Did it just...

"Did you see that?" he asked.

"Your mug sliding away from your hand toward Owen's chair?"

"He still can't leave my coffee alone."

"Make him his own."

"Then Boston and Hyke will want some. I'm not running a café for ghosts."

"Yeah, wouldn't be all that profitable."

"I wonder if we had killed a corejacker, if it would also be haunting the ship."

"Would keep those three occupied."

"Could their ghosts drain the energy from other ghosts?"

"This is getting too complicated. Don't you have constellations to sketch?"

"Okay, okay, getting back to work. Hey, Emma?"

"Yeah?"

"How about we name a few after them? I'm sure Owen would love to have his own constellation."

"Out in the void, far from earth. He'd love that."

"He really should have tried harder to follow step three."

Caron

Every day he woke, said good morning to his wife, made breakfast, checked his mail, and set out to finish another project. The house occasionally needed repair, the fridge needed filling, the yard needed tending, and there was always new music to liven up the day.

"You still trying to use that old rake? It's falling apart." Bob said, standing at the fence.

"It works fine," Daniel responded, tapping the handle.

"You can't see where you're going."

"I can feel. The leaves are over here and the stones outlining the flower bed are right here." He tapped his shoe against them. "Easy."

"What if something moves? Critters move things all the time. Those pesky kids down the road like tormenting people with their antics, maybe they'll move things around to watch you fumble."

"You'd just be laughing alongside them."

"So?"

"They don't mess with me. I bake for them. Nothing tames wild children like a fresh sugar cookie."

"Another activity you shouldn't be doing. Hot stoves are dangerous."

"Why are you always trying to be so restrictive?"

Rhonda laughed. "You two going to have this argument every time you try to work on your lawn?"

"I got shit to do," Daniel said, continuing to rake leaves into a large pile.

"If you fall on that thing and get impaled by those uneven metal tines," Bob started, "I'm going to laugh at you and tell your kids you died from stubbornness. What happened to those rules you told them to follow? Can't follow them yourself?"

"The first two are about space exploration, Bob. The only one I can follow is step three: don't die."

"Well so far, you've only almost died four times since they've been gone. Rhonda's tractor, Antonio's weird dogs, that broken, rusty old shovel that got you sick, and the time you fell down the stairs at that parade last month. Maybe you should tell them about that in your next video."

"Still waiting for their reply."

Bob tapped something against Daniel's shoulder. "Got it from the post this morning. Thought I'd hand deliver it so you couldn't listen to it without me."

"Then get on with it," Rhonda said.

Daniel followed the two inside, sat in his favorite chair, and listened to the voices of his children.

"Hey Dad, good to see you."

Damien sounds well. He's excited about something.

"Loved the song, Bob," Emma said. "Miss hanging around the campfire listening to you and Rhonda singing, having a good time. Hope she's doing well."

Rhonda smiled. "We haven't done that in so long."

Damien spoke again. "We've had quite a few adventures since our last recording. Emma hurt her leg again. Surprising, I know. I'm sure you'll hear about it on the news soon. We ended up getting invaded by an alien race. We didn't even know they were on our ship at first. Crazy looking things..."

A slight pain grew in Daniel's chest. A faint ringing in his ears accompanied by the ever-looming fear. He knew where they were, what they did, and how much they loved it. He knew they were pushing boundaries for science and the betterment of humanity, but his heart would always ache when they spoke of the trials he couldn't help them through, the pains he wasn't able to prevent, and the sorrows he wasn't around for to be a shoulder to cry on.

"We're doing alright now," Damien continued. "Found a way to contain them, found the other ship. Research is having a field day."

"Eli hasn't slept a wink," Emma added.

"Still following your rules. Currently back on base, relaxing and enjoying not fighting for our lives. Sophie's with us."

"Hello," she said.

She's recording with them, I bet I won, Daniel thought, getting ready to grin at Bob. *He was sitting to the left of me, I think... Damn eyes.*

"She's Emma's girlfriend now," Damien said. "Old Bob owes you ten bucks."

"Darn," Bob said, handing over the money. "You know your kids."

Daniel stashed it in his pocket. "You just like trying to take my money."

"Can't take Rhonda's, she'd beat me up."

"I can still win in a fight. I won the last one."

"That was thirty years ago," Rhonda reminded. "Shush and listen."

"Damien's not exactly lonely, either, "Emma continued.

Damien spoke again. "Yeah, well...I've started seeing someone. Officially it's against the rules. You know how Asrocore is. Her name's London. We've told you about her before. She's our programmer. Really smart. I think you'd like her."

"He'd probably like me more," another voice said.

"That's her twin brother, Kenneth. Don't mind him, he's just sour because he's single. What's up?"

"Emma has been requested in the training department," Kenneth responded. "Front wants her to lecture a class on surviving an encounter with corejackers."

"This should be fun."

"Gotta go, Dad," Emma said. "Time to lecture new recruits about step three."

The recording stopped.

Bob tapped Daniel's shoulder. "Looks like your kids both got smart partners. They have better taste than your wife."

"My wife had great taste. I'm good at fixing things and at putting up with you."

"Then go work with your kids, I bet they have things you can fix without functioning eyes."

"I can fix things better than you can."

Rhonda interrupted. "Emma's doing training lectures now. Damn. Already in charge of so much."

"I bet she's hating it," Bob added. "She's always been more of a go out and do things kind of girl, not sit and talk about them. At least she has a good vocabulary for it. Wonder if she's using all those fancy words Caron taught her."

Daniel sighed. "I remember all of them as well."

"Never liked getting a lecture from that woman. Even in her teens she would confuse us with her extra words. All you had back then was good hair."

"I still have good hair."

Rhonda stood and walked toward the door. "I'm going to head to the club and update everyone."

"Bring back some fried zucchini," Bob said. "Haven't had that in a while."

Daniel waved his arm. "Go with her and get some yourself."

"And leave you alone to do more dangerous activities?"

"I've been maintaining that yard myself for years."

"Fine, fine, but if you die, Caron's going to lecture your ghost with her fancy diction and expect you to remember what every word means."

"I'm up for the challenge."

"Alright. See you later, old man."

The wind wasn't blowing. The rain didn't fall. He spent the day listening. Skittering critters, falling leaves, the distant rippling of water from the lake, and the occasional bird singing on their way through the sky.

I wonder if they miss any of this. No birds or winds out there. I know I wouldn't like it, though I bet Emma doesn't have as many nightmares. No more thunder. At least I've still got Bob and Rhonda to come over and keep me company when the storms hit.

He no longer needed to close his eyes to picture her face, though he still did. Her eyes were the same dark brown as her children's. Her hair was short. She always wore coveralls over a bright shirt and obnoxiously yellow boots, even in the summer heat. He could still hear her words, her voice as she called to her kids, telling them not to venture too far, singing with Rhonda and Bob around the fire, reciting the dictionary to two troublemakers, and the words that danced across the waters of the lake when she was out on her boat with not a worry in the world.

"Clouds are coming in. Rhonda said it was supposed to rain."

"She's always right," Daniel added, smiling at his wife.

"Better let the kids know. We might want to head back soon."

"I'm sure they know. They always have their eyes up, trying to see stars in the daylight. You think they'll ever get up there?"

"I'm sure they will. I've never seen more determined kids."

"Do you worry about it?"

"No. Space travel is getting safer every day, and those two can handle adventures like that. I'm sure they'll be running their own crews in no time."

"As long as they come back in once piece. The stars have already taken countless lives."

"Yet we still watch them with stupefaction every night." She looked up. "They'd be able to see them far clearer out there."

"You going to run away with them?"

"And leave you alone with Bob? You two act more married than we do."

"He the only thing keeping you from leaving me for the skies?"

"Verisimilarly..."

He laughed. "Better get used to making breakfast for only myself."

"If you get lonely, look outside, watch the stars, no matter where you are they'll stun you with their beauty. Nothing is a greater distraction than the stars."

He opened his eyes and turned toward the window, imagining the sight of thousands of bright speckles in a dark sky. His mind explored the possibilities of what fantastical constellations his children were seeing. Brightly colored galaxies and flashing suns ready to brighten the skies of endless planets.

"You were always right, Caron."

If you enjoyed this book, check out its sequel.
The Shadows of Charlotte Grace.

About the author

Rivara Fall is an author with a passion for peculiar things. Her books fall into several genres including mystery, fantasy, lgbt, sci-fi, romance, and adventure. Born and raised in western Washington, she enjoys rainy weather, playing video games, and spending time with her mischievous pets. Her passions include theatre, science, and art.

If you're interested in seeing her upcoming books, or artistic designs from her stories, you can visit – rivarafall.com

www.ingramcontent.com/pod-product-compliance
Lightning Source LLC
Chambersburg PA
CBHW031055020726
47495CB00007B/1891